Campfire Secrets

by
Kathi Daley

This book is a work of fiction. Names, characters, places, and incidents either are products of the author's imagination or are used fictitiously. Any resemblance to actual events or locales or persons, living or dead, is entirely coincidental.

Chapter 1

Lizzy's daughter, Grace, is missing. The last thing Sheriff Sam Stone had said to us before running from the marina toward his truck echoed through my mind as I helped Ryder West and his team secure the sailboat following the last race of the season before the regatta. I supposed we should have seen it coming. Not only was Grace a beautiful sixteen-year-old girl with long blond hair, blue eyes, and a petite frame, but she was also a surfer and an artist, which meant that she was a perfect fit for the physical profile Sam had come up with to help us understand the pattern of missing girls over the past quarter of a century.

"Kelly, can you grab that line," Ryder called out to me after Sam had left to respond to the call.

"I got it," I called back, shaking myself from my trance. Today, I was part of Ryder's official sailing crew since Cliff Brown, one of the regulars, was out of town. I'd been honored to be chosen to fill Cliff's role, and really wanted to do my part despite my preoccupation. "Do you need help with the sails?"

"I got em," Nina Collins, the fourth member of Ryder's team, called out.

I secured the line as Ryder had asked, and then set about wiping down all the salty surfaces while my good friend, Diane "Quinn" Quinby, helped Nina tie everything down. I knew that what I was doing was important, but it was hard to focus on my chores given the nature of the 911 call Sam had received when we'd returned to the harbor. Was Lizzy's daughter, Grace, really missing? I supposed it was possible that she'd simply taken off with friends, but given everything else I knew, I realized that it was just as likely she was trapped somewhere, scared and afraid.

"Now that we've pretty much finished up here, should we do something to help Sam?" I asked Ryder after he joined me on the bow.

"I'm not sure what we can do," he answered. "Sam knows we're here if he needs us, but he's the cop, and we're the civilians, so at this point, I think all we can do is to wait until we hear from him."

I blew out a slow breath of frustration. "I guess you're right, but I've gotten pretty wrapped up in the mystery of the missing girls since I've been on the island, and I feel like I should have seen this coming. I feel responsible for what happened."

Ryder turned and looked me in the eye. He reached out a hand and ran a finger along my jaw, brushing away a wisp of hair that had fallen from my ponytail before answering. "You aren't responsible for what happened, assuming that something has indeed happened," he spoke slowly as if to ensure that

I really understood what he was saying. "At this point, we can only guess at what's going on. It's entirely possible that Sam was called in to deal with a simple case of teen rebellion."

"But what if it isn't teen rebellion?" I asked as the tension I'd been suppressing knotted in my stomach. "What if Grace *is* the blond-haired blue-eyed sixteen-year-old girl who fits the pattern of missing girls for the summer of twenty-twenty?"

"Then, we'll find her."

"You can't know that for sure," I pointed out, as fingers of panic clawed at my chest, causing my heart to pound at an abnormal rate. "You can't know that Grace is okay. You can't know that she isn't dead, or even worse, trapped and terrified."

He pulled me against his chest, wrapping his arms around me. "You're right. I can't know any of that. But I can hope. And I can pray. And I can put my faith in Sam to find her."

"I'm just so scared." I squeezed my arms tightly around his waist, allowing the steady rhythm of his heartbeat beneath my ear to calm me. I'm not sure how long we stood there, taking comfort in each other's arms. Probably only seconds, but it seemed longer. Eventually, I took a slow, calming breath and stepped back.

"Okay?" he asked, looking deeply into my eyes.

I nodded. Deep down inside, I knew that Ryder was right. Panicking wouldn't help anyone. I'd been trained to look at a situation with logic rather than emotion, which, I realized, was the best thing I could do at this point. It wasn't like I knew Grace all that well. I knew her mother, who I'd gone to high school with, and I knew her father, who I'd dated in high school, but the first time I met Grace was a few days ago. The level of fear I'd let consume me really couldn't be justified. I supposed the feelings of helplessness I'd been struggling with since I'd had to watch my sister die, unable to pull her back to the world of the living after months of trying, had somehow become wrapped up in my concern for Grace. Not that I wouldn't be concerned for a missing teen no matter the situation, but the panic I felt at this moment seemed to come from out of nowhere. I took a deep breath, took a moment to acknowledge the damage Kayla's death had done to my sense of security and willed myself to relax.

"Does someone want to catch me up?" Nina asked after joining Ryder and me at the front of the boat. "I know it's rude to listen in on the conversations of those around me, but I happened to overhear enough of your conversation to really fuel my curiosity, and I've been wondering what it was that caused Sam to bolt out of here without even helping to tie up."

I glanced at Ryder, who stepped aside to make room for Quinn, who'd also walked up to join us.

"I guess you know that Quinn and I are here to visit Carrie Davidson, who we've known since we were children," I started.

"Yes," Nina replied. "Carrie told me that she'd been a full-time resident when you were all kids and that you, Quinn, and Nora had been summer-only residents who'd gotten to know each other and became friends.

"Basically," I answered, although we'd been a lot closer than Nina made it sound. "We also had another friend, Peggy. She grew up with us, and we were all close, but when she was sixteen, she disappeared without a trace."

"What do you mean without a trace?" Nina asked.

"She took a walk down the beach during a party and was never seen again," Quinn filled her in.

Nina gasped. "How awful. And you think this missing girl Sam had to leave to deal with is somehow related?"

"We aren't sure," I answered. "Sam noticed a pattern after he took over when Sheriff Renshaw retired. Apparently, after Peggy went missing in nineteen ninety-five, other blond-haired blue-eyed sixteen-year-olds went missing during the twenty-five years that followed. Some were reported to be runaways, while others were classified as missing persons, but the pattern seems pretty consistent. A new girl has gone missing every five years."

"The last girl on Sam's list went missing in two thousand fifteen, so we've suspected for a while that the next girl would go missing this year," Ryder added.

"And you think the next girl is this Grace?" Nina asked.

"We think there's a possibility that Grace is the next girl in the series," Quinn said.

"Have any of the girls ever been found?" Nina asked.

I shook my head. "Not until Veronica Smith washed up on the beach."

Nina frowned. "Does the girl they found dead on the beach fit this pattern?"

"Yes, she does," I confirmed.

Nina had only lived on the island for a few years, so she wouldn't have been around when Veronica went missing in two thousand fifteen. I could see that she was struggling to wrap her head around this whole thing.

"So, what do you think happens to the girls after they disappear?" Nina finally asked.

"We aren't sure," I answered. "Until Veronica washed up on the beach, I personally assumed that Peggy had been killed and her body disposed of either in the sea or somewhere where it would never be found. But now that we know that Veronica, who'd been missing for five years, was alive until a few hours before her body was found, I guess I may need to adjust my assumptions."

"So, do you think your friend from the nineties might still be alive?" Nina asked.

Did I? I hoped that was true, but it had been a quarter of a century. The odds were very much against Peggy still being alive. "I don't know," I finally answered. "It's been a long time since she disappeared, but maybe some of the more recent victims are still alive somewhere. The problem is that we have no idea where Veronica has been for the past five years. Sam is working on some clues, but so far, they aren't coming together."

"Wow," Nina said. "When Sam announced his departure, I could see that the three of you were upset, but I had no idea how upset you must be. Not knowing where this girl has been for five years or what happened to her before her body washed up on the beach must be terrifying. Are you close to the girl who disappeared today?"

"No," Quinn answered. "Not really. We knew Grace's parents back when we were teens summering here, but we haven't stayed in touch."

"Like Quinn, I hadn't seen Grace's parents since I summered here as a teen, but I ran into her mother at the Perfect Tan Surfing Competition, where her three daughters were contestants," I added.

"So the Grace who's missing is the Grace who won the competition?" Nina paused, lowering her eyes as if the severity of the situation really hit home. "I hadn't put that together. I've seen her around. I've even watched her surf a few times. She's very talented."

"She's one of the best I've ever seen," Quinn agreed.

"I hope she's okay," Nina said, raising her eyes to meet Quinn's. "Maybe she isn't in any sort of trouble. Maybe she just celebrated too hard after winning the competition and is sleeping it off at a friend's."

Boy, I hoped that was true.

"Why don't the three of you head over to the beach," Ryder suggested. "The race has been over for a while, so Carrie must be wondering where we all are. I need to run Baja home, so I'll just meet you there."

Nina announced that she wasn't going to join us at the beach this week since she had plans to meet up with her fiancé, so she said goodbye to Ryder and then headed toward her car. Quinn and I confirmed that we would do as Ryder suggested and head over to meet up with Carrie, so we moved toward the parking area and piled into my Mercedes. Once we were underway, Quinn texted Sam and asked him to call when he had a chance. I was sure he would think to call even without a text to remind him, but both Quinn and I were more than just mildly interested in what was going on.

When we arrived at the beach, we immediately noticed Carrie standing next to the huge bright purple and lime green umbrella she'd brought. She was waving her arms as if to get our attention, but truth be told, I'd recognize that umbrella anywhere. Carrie had always been one to *go colorful or go home*, and it seemed that while many facets of her personality had changed after her husband of twenty years had left her for another woman, her tendency to stand out had stayed much the same.

"Did you hear?" Carrie asked the minute we arrived with our beach bags.

"Hear what?" I asked, figuring it was unlikely Carrie had heard about Grace.

"Lizzy Chambers' daughter, Grace, is missing."

I glanced at Quinn. She looked as surprised as I felt. "I did know that," I answered. "Sam had a message when we got back to the marina after the race. But how did you hear?"

"I called Lizzy," Carrie explained. "I wanted to congratulate her on Grace's victory. She told me that she hadn't seen Grace since she'd left for a party at the beach last evening."

I grabbed a bottle of water from the ice chest before asking the next question on my mind. "So, what exactly did Lizzy tell you?"

Carrie sat down in the lime green beach chair she'd placed under the umbrella. Quinn and I both sat down on two of the other five chairs Carrie had brought. Eventually, Carrie spoke. "According to Lizzy, the whole thing started after Grace won the surfing competition. As we'd discussed earlier, Lizzy had really hoped that Hope would win this year since a loss most likely would mean an end to Hope's participation in the competition."

It was true that if you weren't a contender by the time you reached your twenty-first birthday, you probably weren't going to attract the attention of sponsors, so a lot of surfers dropped out at that point.

Carrie continued. "Lizzy admitted that even though Grace won and she was happy for her to a degree, she was disappointed that Hope didn't come in high enough to earn a medal. Apparently, Grace picked up on this and was angry and hurt that her own mother didn't support her. The two exchanged words, which led to tears and hurt feelings all around, so when Grace announced that she was leaving to attend a party on the beach with her friends, Lizzy let her go. When Grace didn't come home last night, Lizzy figured that Grace was even madder about the sponsorship than she thought, and assumed she'd spent the night with a girlfriend."

"Hang on," Quinn said. "What's this about a sponsorship? I thought Grace was mad because her mom wasn't happy for her."

"She was," Carrie said. "But apparently the fight they'd had was really over the fact that Grace had been offered this huge deal to go pro, which is something she really wanted but Lizzy didn't. I think the fact that Lizzy was actually disappointed Grace had won added fuel to the fire."

"Go on," I said. "Grace tried to talk to Lizzy about this amazing opportunity, but Lizzy shot her down. I've been there. I know how frustrating it can be to have a parent stand in the way of something, which at that moment, is the most important thing in the world to you. I also get where Lizzy is coming from. Grace is still in high school."

"Exactly," Carrie said. "Anyway, mom and daughter fought and then daughter left to go to the party she'd already been planning to attend. When Grace didn't come home, Lizzy initially assumed she'd stayed over with a friend. But when she didn't come home by this afternoon, Lizzy got worried and began to call around. According to Grace's best friends, Grace was in a mood last night when she arrived at the party. After she'd been there half an hour or so, she told everyone that she was just going to head home, but she never arrived there. Her car isn't at the beach, so Lizzy assumes she left the party, but as of the point when I spoke to Lizzy, no one knew where she'd gone after she left the party."

"This is an island. I'm sure her car is somewhere," I said. "Unless she took the ferry this morning, but even then, the ferry has security cameras that record all the cars as they load and unload."

"I'm sure Sammy will think of that," Quinn said. "He's probably got the crew from the Sea Haven office looking at the tapes as we speak."

"I'm sure Quinn's right," Carrie said. "Maybe Ryder will know more about what's going on. Did he say when he'd be here?"

"He shouldn't be long," I answered. "He had a few little things to finish up, and then he was going to run Baja home. I think he mentioned that there were a few things he wanted to grab from the house as well. I guess we should assume that Sam won't make it."

"Probably not," Quinn agreed. "Unless, of course, they find Grace safe and sound at a friend's."

"Let's hope that's true," Carrie replied.

"I think I'll text him again, just to be sure," Quinn said. "I'd hate to go ahead and eat without him if he's on his way."

Quinn texted Sam, not really expecting to hear from him right away, so I think we were all surprised when he called back.

"I wasn't expecting you to get back to me right away," Quinn said. "But I'm glad you did. Carrie and Kelly are here. Is it okay if I put you on speaker?"

He must have indicated that it was okay since that's what Quinn did.

"Did you find her?" Quinn asked as soon as the phone was switched over.

"No." Sam sounded frustrated. "I've spoken to several of her friends, and no one has seen her. Lizzy is making me a list of other friends to talk to, and Grace's best friend, Loretta, is making me a list of everyone she can remember being at the party. I still haven't given up on the idea that Grace might be intentionally hiding out after the argument with her mother, but I'm not holding out a lot of hope at this point."

"Is there anything we can do to help?" Quinn asked.

"No. Buford and I are going to talk to the friends on the list as well as those who were at the party. The Sea Haven office has two deputies out looking for Grace's car. If she's still on this island, we'll find her. If not…"

"Find out if Wilson Montgomery is still on the island," I suggested. "I have a bad feeling about the guy."

"Yeah, you mentioned that when we talked before," Sam said. "I'll look into it. I also called

Moon. He didn't answer his cell, but I left a message. One of the deputies from the Sea Haven office is going to see if he can track him down."

Moon was a local artist who summered on Shipwreck Island but lived in a mansion near Carmel the rest of the year. He'd known all the girls who'd gone missing since Peggy's disappearance, which made him a suspect in my mind, but Sam had talked to him and didn't seem to think he was the guy we were after.

Sam paused as someone called out his name in the background.

"Listen, I have to go," he said.

"Call me later," Quinn said. "When you can. No matter how late it is."

"Okay, I will."

With that, he hung up.

Ryder pulled up in his truck as Sam disconnected the call. When he arrived at our umbrella, we brought him up to speed. After a bit of discussion, we decided we weren't really in the mood for a cookout and bonfire, so we all headed to the rental. Once we arrived, Ryder grilled some burgers, Carrie transferred the salads we'd brought to go with the burgers from the ice chests to the counter, and Quinn and I opened a couple of bottles of wine.

"So I heard from Nora while you were all sailing," Carrie said after we'd settled around the patio table with our meal.

"How's she doing?" I asked. Nora Hargrove was the fourth friend, along with Carrie, Quinn, and me who'd come to Shipwreck Island for a reunion in honor of Peggy, who'd been missing from our lives for twenty-five years but was far from forgotten. Nora and her husband, Matt, had been going through a rough patch after their youngest went off to college, so their oldest son, Denver, had decided to kidnap them in order to force them to talk things out and deal with their problems.

"She seemed fine," Carrie answered. "She said that after she arrived at the beach house Denver rented for her and Matt this week, he sat them both down and told them to figure it out. She said he was quite forceful in his delivery and told them in no uncertain terms that his family was the most important thing to him, and he was not willing to live with a situation where his parents were anything less than totally committed to one another. She admitted to being nervous at first, but she could see that Matt was taking this retreat seriously, and she intended to as well. She had real hope in her tone, which is a big improvement from her tone before Denver got involved and took the bull by the horns."

"I really hope they work it out," I said. "Matt and Nora have always seemed like the perfect couple."

"I agree," Carrie said. "I can understand how raising four children might have caused them to drift apart, but now that the children are all adults and they have the house to themselves, they just need to adjust to putting the needs of each other ahead of the needs of anyone else in their lives."

Quinn glanced in my direction. "And that is only one example of why I am single. I can do what I want when I want, and I never have to worry about another person."

"Maybe, but you do have a job to worry about," Carrie pointed out. "A very demanding job."

"For now," she sighed.

"For now?" Carrie asked. "Are you thinking about quitting?"

"I don't think there's been a single day in the past three years that I haven't thought about quitting. That doesn't mean I will, but I do think about it."

After we finished our meal, Quinn and Carrie both went up to their suites. Carrie liked to watch television in the evenings before going to bed, and Quinn announced that she really did need to return some of the calls and emails she'd been avoiding. In my opinion, my friends had both made up excuses to head upstairs so that Ryder and I could have some alone time together.

"So, are you on for our run tomorrow morning?" I asked Ryder after the others had left.

"I am," he answered. "Tomorrow is Monday, so I have my shot clinic, but I'll have time to run first as long as I don't have any emergencies. Let's plan to meet as usual, and if something comes up, I'll call or text."

"How is that patient doing that you were so concerned about?" I asked about a dog who'd required two surgeries and several days in the hospital last week.

"He's doing great. It was touch and go for a while, but he went home yesterday, and I expect a full recovery once the stitches heal."

I turned my chair slightly so I could look out over the sea. It was a gorgeous night, but I couldn't quite bring myself to relax and enjoy it. "I wonder how Sam is doing. I assume if Grace had been found, he would have called or texted, so I guess she's still missing."

Ryder wove his fingers through mine. "I'm sure Sam is doing everything he can, but these things aren't always solved with a few interviews or phone calls. If she has been taken or if she voluntarily left and doesn't want to be found, we might not know anything for certain for days or even longer."

"Do you think she would take off of her own free will and worry everyone the way she has?" I asked.

"I don't know Grace well, but based on what I do know, I would say probably not. But sixteen is a tricky age. I bet if you ask Sam, he'd tell you that there are more cases where the teen simply takes off in a snit than there are cases where the missing teen was actually in any sort of danger."

"Yeah, but we have a unique situation going on here."

"Yes. We do," Ryder admitted.

Quinn came down a short time later to let us know that she'd spoken to Sam. They still hadn't found Grace, but they had found her car abandoned along a dirt road just north of the marina in Hidden Harbor. The road was really more of a trail that was used mostly by equestrians, although the occasional hiker or mountain biker could be found in the area as well.

"So does Sam think Grace went to this location for some reason and disappeared from there, or does he think she disappeared from somewhere else, and the car was moved and abandoned there?" Ryder asked Quinn.

She sat down on a chair near where we were sitting. "He didn't know. The car is going to be towed to the impound lot. The crime scene guys from the county will come out to look for fingerprints as well as other physical evidence. If Grace was kidnapped and the person who kidnapped her moved the car from wherever she was taken to the dirt trail where it was found, maybe they'll find evidence inside the car that will help to identify the person who took her."

"So I guess the idea that Grace simply took off and is staying with a friend is no longer on the table," I said.

"I would think that to be a factual statement," Quinn answered. "I guess, deep down, I suspected that was the case from the beginning, but it does help to know for certain what Sam is dealing with."

I supposed that was true, but I had to admit that with confirmation of kidnapping came an intensified feeling of stress and uncertainty. "Did Sam mention whether or not he'd been able to speak to Wilson Montgomery?" I asked.

"He called him, but Wilson has already returned to Montgomery Island. Sam asked if he would be willing to come back to Shipwreck Island for questioning, and he said he would, but he wouldn't commit to when."

"Can't Sam just go to the island and talk to him?" Ryder asked.

Quinn answered. "Not if Wilson is unwilling to grant him access to the island. Without a warrant, he won't be able to simply force his way onto the island, and without a compelling reason to suspect Wilson or someone else on the island of wrongdoing, he'll never get a warrant. At this point, all he can really do is hope that Wilson will cooperate. If he won't, Sam is going to have a rough go of it. Gavin Montgomery is a very wealthy man with a whole lot of influence. I learned the hard way that if he doesn't want to be gotten to, there is no way to get to him, and I assume the same is true of his son."

"We need physical evidence linking Wilson to Grace's disappearance," I said.

"We do, but I really doubt that getting that physical evidence is going to be easy," Quinn said. "He might have been careless and left fingerprints in the car if he moved it himself, but short of that, I'm afraid that Sam has an uphill battle ahead of him if it was Wilson who took her."

Ryder glanced at his watch. "I really should go." He glanced at me. "I'll see you at our regular meeting spot in the morning."

"Okay," I said, looking up at him.

He bent down, kissed me briefly on the lips, and then headed toward the drive where he'd left his truck.

"I didn't mean to interrupt," Quinn said.

"You didn't interrupt. We were actually talking about Grace before you came down."

Quinn moved over to the chair Ryder had vacated since it was closer to me, and it afforded a better view of the sea than the chair she'd been sitting in.

"I pulled up some aerial photos of the island," Quinn informed me. "There are a lot of buildings on the island, and it's pretty much impossible to know for certain what any of them are used for, with the exception of the main house, which sprawls in every direction, and the helicopter bay."

"How many buildings are there?" I asked.

"A lot. There are long buildings that look like they could be either warehouses or dormitory-style housing for the island employees, and there are other buildings that look as if they could be used for storage or manufacturing, but the building I'm most interested in is a large square structure that looks like a greenhouse."

I raised a brow. "A greenhouse? As in the sort of place where one might grow Kadupul flowers and opium poppies?"

"Perhaps. There's no way to know what's being grown inside based on the aerial view, but the existence of such a building does seem significant based on what we know. If the greenhouse does possess Kadupul flowers and opium poppies and we can link them back to the seeds and flower petal on Veronica Smith's body, that might give Sam enough cause to get the warrant he needs to really take a look around."

"I agree, but how do we prove the greenhouse has these two specific flowers?" I asked.

"Seems to me that someone is going to need to figure out a way to sneak onto the island and take a look."

"Someone like us?" I asked.

She nodded. "I know I tried to get on the island in the past and was unsuccessful, but I was just starting out as a journalist and had a limited playbook. But now, I think there might be a way. It will be risky, and planning will be key, but if we're careful, I think we can sneak onto the island and get a look at the greenhouse. It's near the back of the property, and I doubt it's as highly guarded as the house and warehouses."

"Okay, I'm in," I decided without really taking the time to think things over. "When do we go?"

"We'll need to go at night, and it would be best to go on a night where the moon is blocked by clouds or fog. We'll need a boat and paddle or surfboards, as well as a waterproof camera and full-length black wetsuits with hoods."

"So, your plan is to paddle onto the island?"

She nodded. "I think that if we approach from the backside on a dark night, we should be able to sneak onto the island without being seen. A boat can't access the island from the back due to the rocks, so my plan is to have someone take us as close to the island as they can and then wait for us in the boat while we paddle in."

"We should do this without Sam's knowledge," I said. "He's a cop, and what we're planning is illegal. He'd have no choice but to stop us. It's best if he's completely out of the loop."

"Agreed," Quinn said. "We can have Carrie or Ryder man the boat."

"Let's ask Carrie. Ryder might be risking his political career if we get caught, and Gavin Montgomery decides to make an issue of it. I have nothing to lose, not really. Carrie doesn't have a career to protect, but you do. Are you sure you want to risk it?"

Quinn laughed. "Totally. This wouldn't even be the most dangerous thing I've done this month. Trust me. I've got this."

I nodded. "Okay. I'm in."

"I want to study the maps and aerial images a bit more before we attempt our approach. And we should look at the weather forecast to pick the best night as well. The darker, the better. Once we have a solid plan, we'll talk to Carrie, line up a boat, paddle or surfboards, and whatever else we need. Then when the time is right, we'll head out and get Sammy the physical evidence he needs to get the warrant he must realize is going to be necessary to find out if Grace is on that island or not.

Chapter 2

As planned, I met Ryder the next morning for our run. Quinn and I had discussed the fact that it was going to be important to keep to our regular schedule as much as possible as we came up with our plan to sneak onto the island and have a look around. We planned to talk to Carrie this morning over coffee and bagels. Once we determined whether or not she was on board, we'd move forward outlining our next steps. We figured it would take a couple of days to get everything ready before we could make our move. Quinn had a friend in Naval Intelligence who'd helped her acquire the intel she'd needed for stories she'd worked on in the past. She planned to call him today and ask him if he could get his hands on better photos of the island and surrounding sea. It would be important to find the best place to approach.

In the meantime, we planned to carry out the tasks we'd already put into play. The previous evening, Carrie had told Ryder that she, Quinn, and I had plans to spend the afternoon at her new condo, putting things away and waiting for her new furniture to be delivered. Quinn felt that if at all possible, we should stick to that plan. It felt wrong to lie to Ryder. I supposed that technically not telling him what we planned to do wasn't lying since the subject had never come up, but when he mentioned a concert later in the week, I'd been forced to tell him that I might have plans with Quinn and Carrie and would need to get back to him. Of course, what I really meant was that I needed to figure out which night we were going to execute our plan to access the island before I could make plans with him or anyone else.

"Is everything okay?" Ryder asked as we jogged along the hard sand near the waterline. "You seem sort of distracted."

"I'm fine," I said. "Well, I suppose fine isn't really accurate. I guess I've been thinking about Grace. I can't help picturing her in all sorts of terrifying situations, and it isn't sitting right to feel so powerless to help her."

"I know what you mean. She's been on my mind a lot as well. Maybe Sam will have news today. Good news."

"Have you spoken to him?"

"No," Ryder answered. "I'm going to call him after I get back to the boathouse. I didn't want to call him too early in the event he was up late."

"Are you planning to make a statement about the case? As mayor of the island, I mean."

"I'm sure I'll get a call from the local newspaper today asking for a statement. I'm sure Sam will as well. One of the reasons I want to speak to him beforehand is so we can ensure that we're on the same page before either of us says anything."

"That sounds like a good idea. I'm hoping that Sam will find something linking Wilson to Grace, which should be his ticket to access to the island."

"You seem really certain that Wilson is the man behind all the disappearances."

"I won't say that I'm certain, but I do have a gut feeling. There's something about the guy that creeps me out."

"He is an odd sort of fellow, but I've spoken to him on occasion, and I certainly never picked up the serial killer vibe. In fact, I've found him to be mature and level headed, even when it comes to subjects he may feel strongly about."

"He keeps women here on the island. More than one from what I've heard."

"Wilson certainly isn't the only man of means to offer financial support to women he occasionally enjoys an intimate relationship with, and doing so certainly doesn't mean he is guilty of wrongdoing," Ryder pointed out.

"Maybe, but the guy still seems shifty to me."

Ryder slowed as a man with two dogs jogged toward us from the opposite direction. Baja was an obedient dog who stayed next to Ryder as we ran, but it wasn't unusual for dogs to approach him, as the two dogs had today. Normally, when that occurred, Ryder allowed Baja to say hi before calling him to his side and continuing on his way.

"That guy looked familiar," I said after Ryder greeted the man, Baja greeted his dogs, and everyone moved on.

"His name is Tim Newton. He's lived on the island for a long time. Probably since you used to summer here."

"Newton? Is that the same Tim Newton, whose father worked as a video game developer?"

"That'd be him. When you lived here before, he was still in college, but he has since graduated and developed his own career in software development. He has a house on the island, but he lives full-time on the Bay."

"It sounds like he's done well for himself."

"He has," Ryder agreed. "He started off developing video games like his father but has since branched out. Most recently, he partnered up with a guy who used to work for the Department of Justice and has branched into high-end cybersecurity systems."

"Wow. I'm impressed. It seemed like the two of you are friends."

"We are. Tim has done very well for himself, but he's also a regular guy. We get together for drinks every now and then, mostly to discuss his willingness to participate in some of the community projects that depend on donations."

"So you aren't only a politician, but a mooch as well," I teased.

"For the right cause, you bet I am."

After Ryder and I worked our way back around to our starting point, he kissed me goodbye, and then we headed back to our respective residences. Carrie and Quinn were talking on the deck when I arrived, so I grabbed a mug of coffee and joined them.

"It's a beautiful day," I said, sitting down with my friends.

"It is," Carrie agreed. "Although I'm having a hard time appreciating it with everything that's been going on."

"Any news about Grace?" I asked.

Carrie shook her head. "Not a word." She glanced at Quinn. "Quinn tells me that the two of you think Wilson Montgomery is involved and are planning to prove it."

"We've talked about him as a suspect before," I reminded Carrie.

"We have. As recently as last night, in fact. What we didn't talk about was a plan the two of you hatched to sneak onto the island behind Sam's back."

I took a sip of my coffee. "I take it you're against the idea."

"I think it sounds dangerous. Why not fill Sam in on your plan? Why all the secrecy?"

"Like I told you," Quinn said, "Sam is the sheriff, and therefore he's bound by the law and certain limitations and procedures when it comes to gathering information. If he ventures outside those limitations and procedures, then anything he might stumble across which could prove that Wilson Montgomery has been holding girls against their will for the past quarter of a century, will be inadmissible in court."

"He needs to go through channels," I added. "We don't. The only way he's going to get access to the island is if he finds enough evidence to convince a judge to issue a warrant. At this point, all any of us have is a hunch, and given Gavin Montgomery's wealth and political clout, I don't think a hunch is going to do it."

"You might get caught," Carrie pointed out.

"We might," Quinn agreed. "But I've done time behind bars in the past for being where I wasn't supposed to be. I have connections, and I always find my way out of any mess I get myself into."

"What if you aren't arrested?" Carrie asked. "What if you're shot by Montgomery's security staff? Do you have connections that can bring you back from the dead?"

I could see that Carrie was getting upset, and that was not the way to get her cooperation. I jumped in. "We aren't saying we are definitely doing anything," I pointed out. "We're just talking about it. Not only do we want to find out what happened to Peggy, but even more importantly, we want to find Grace. She's just a kid. If she is being held somewhere against her will, she must be terrified."

I could see that Carrie's resistance had begun to waver.

"We have good reason to believe that Wilson is involved," I continued. "We know he was at the surfing competition this past weekend. We all saw him there. We also all saw him talking to Grace. Granted, we witnessed him speak to other surfers as well, but Grace is the one who won the competition, so she was the one to draw the most attention."

"And she fits the profile," Quinn reminded her.

"And she fits the profile," I seconded. "Lizzy told Sam that Grace had been offered a sponsorship if she wanted to go pro. She told us that she and Grace fought about this before Grace went off to her party. The situation obviously upset Grace. What if the sponsorship was actually offered by Wilson as a way to get Grace to meet with him in private? What if he used that offer to lure her onto his boat? What if, once she was on the boat, he tied her up or locked her in one of the rooms or maybe had one of his crew watch her while he disposed of her car?"

"Or maybe he paid someone to dispose of her car," Quinn said, offering a more viable option.

"Montgomery Island is a fortress," I added. "There's no way on unless you're invited, and once on the island, I've heard that you need permission to leave. If Wilson has been using his money to talk these girls into meeting with him, once he got them on the island, they'd have no way to leave unless he allowed them to."

Carrie didn't respond, but I could see she was listening.

"Veronica Smith disappeared after the finals of the same surfing competition Grace disappeared from. Five years before that, the girl we know as Cherry disappeared after winning the exact same competition," I reminded Carrie. "I don't know if Hillary Denton entered the competition, but I do remember someone saying that she surfed. And I have no idea if Gina Baldwin even surfed, or if either girl knew Wilson. What I do know is that Peggy knew Wilson and that she went to a concert with him just eight days before she disappeared."

"Peggy wasn't much of a surfer," Carrie pointed out.

"That's true. If the competition is the link, I suppose I'd have been the target and not Peggy since I won the dang thing."

"Maybe you were the target," Quinn pointed out. "You have blond hair, blue eyes, and a petite frame. You fit the profile perfectly."

"You were even offered a sponsorship," Carrie reminded me.

"Yeah, but not by Wilson or his father. The sponsorship was offered by someone from the Optimal Wave group."

"Maybe you were Wilson's choice, and it actually was Wilson who funded the sponsorship, but you didn't choose to play the game and meet up with him later, so he took Peggy instead," Carrie suggested. "She had blond hair and blue eyes too, so maybe she made an acceptable substitute."

"Did the man you spoke to about the sponsorship ask you to meet him alone?" Carrie asked.

"Sort of," I admitted. "He made the offer, but I told him I would need to talk to my parents. He told me that he would be at the marina until the following morning, and if I decided to take him up on his offer, I could find him there. I went home and talked to my parents, who put an end to my dreams before they even got started. I probably knew they were right on some level, so I went to the party, and that was the end of it. I never saw the guy who made the offer again."

"Wilson was following us around all weekend," Quinn reminded me. "Maybe he'd targeted you, but hadn't figured it all out yet if that was his first kidnapping. Maybe he had been dating Peggy to get close to you, so when she showed up, assuming that's even what happened, he simply took her instead of you."

Talk about a lot to digest. What if Peggy had been taken as some sort of substitute for me? I wasn't sure how I'd live with that if that was what had occurred.

"At this point, we can't prove any of this," Quinn said. "We need to get on that island and look around." She looked at Carrie. "Will you help us?"

She nodded. "Yeah, I'll help. What do you want me to do?"

Chapter 3

I was surprised to see how much Carrie had accomplished since I'd last visited the condo. The kitchen was mostly set up, as was the patio. One of the suites was filled with boxes and furniture from Jessica's bedroom, while the guest room had been set up using Carrie's bedroom set from the old house. Carrie explained that she was having a new bedroom set for the master delivered today, as well as a new sofa and love seat, matching coffee and end tables, a dining table and chairs, and an entry table that she assured me was going to look spectacular and fit perfectly.

"The place is really coming along," I said after poking my head into all the rooms.

"I've been working hard to get it livable as soon as possible," Carrie admitted. "I really can't face going back to the house where I lived with Carl all those years. I want to have the move complete before the summerhouse rental is up, and you all go home."

"Well, I think you've made great strides in that direction," I said.

"Do you know what time the men from the furniture store will be here with your new stuff?" Quinn asked.

"I estimate between noon and three," Carrie answered. "If they came over on the early ferry, it will be closer to noon, but if they took a later ferry, it will be later in the afternoon. They said they'd text once they had a better time estimate."

"I love how the corner window opens up the room," I said. "Not only do you look directly out toward the water and beach through the front window, but the side window in the corner gives you a panorama. Did you ever decide between blinds and drapes?"

"Blinds," Carrie answered. "You made a good point when you said that drapes would obstruct the view."

"Do you have the blinds on order?" I asked.

She nodded. "Nora and I ordered some the day we went shopping."

"Speaking of Nora, I wonder how things are going," Quinn said. "I know she's only been gone one day, but the situation seems like the sort of thing that might either go really well or really poorly."

"I'm sure things will go a little of each way before all is said and done, but I have faith it will all work out in the end," Carrie answered. She glanced out the window. "It looks like Sam is here. Were either of you expecting him to stop by?"

"No," I said.

"I did text him to let him know what we planned to do this afternoon, so he knew we'd be here, but he never mentioned stopping by," Quinn added.

Carrie went to the door and opened it before Sam had a chance to knock. "Come in," she said. "I'm glad you stopped by. I've been looking for an opportunity to show you my new place."

He entered the room. "It's very nice." He looked around a bit. "A perfect location. But I'm afraid I'm not here socially."

Carrie frowned. "What is it? Not Ryder?"

"Ryder is fine," Sam assured her.

"Jessica?"

"Jessica is fine as well," Sam answered. "The reason I'm here has to do with Grace Johnson."

"Did you find her?" I jumped in.

"No, but we did find her cell phone in her car, and we were able to trace the last call she made before the phone was turned off."

"Who'd she call?" I asked.

Sam looked directly at Carrie. "She called Carl."

She gasped, clutching her chest as she did so. "My Carl?"

He nodded.

"Why on earth would Lizzy's daughter, Grace, call Carl? I doubt they even know each other."

Sam answered. "I'm not sure, but I am interested in asking Carl that exact question. The problem is that he's not picking up his phone and he's not home. I went to his office, and his receptionist told me that she hadn't seen him since Friday. Carl keeps his own schedule, so she didn't know where he might be, but she did say that as far as she knew, he hadn't planned to come in this week."

"When you say Grace called Carl, did she call his office, his home, or his personal cell?" Quinn asked.

"Personal cell. Of course, his cell number is on ads all over town, so it wouldn't have been hard to get. It looks like the call occurred after Grace left the party on Saturday night." Sam tightened his lips. "Do you have any idea where Carl might be, or how I might be able to get ahold of him?"

Carrie slowly shook her head. The poor thing looked shell shocked. "I have no idea. Have you spoken to Miranda?"

Miranda was the woman Carl had left Carrie for. The woman Carl now lived with and would most likely marry.

"She wasn't at the house when I went by, and her phone went straight to voice mail when I called. I'll keep trying. If for some reason you hear from Carl, I need you to ask him to call me," Sam said.

She lowered her head. "Yeah. I will. And if you hear from him, will you let me know? I'm sure everything is fine, but I still can't help but worry."

Sam nodded. "I wouldn't worry too much at this point, but I will call and let you know if I manage to track him down."

"Is there any other news in the Grace Johnson missing persons case?" I asked Sam while I had his attention.

Sam hesitated and then answered. "The crime scene guys were unable to find fingerprints inside Grace's car that didn't belong to either Grace, her friends, or her family. There wasn't any blood, which is good, nor was there any physical evidence to point us in a direction. We have the phone, but it didn't tell us much. There were calls to friends earlier in the day, which I've been able to confirm, a call to the bowling alley, and then the call to Carl."

"And you didn't find anything that would tell you how the car ended up where it did?" I asked.

"No. We really have no idea why the car was left there. We're following up on a few leads."

"Hopefully, those will pan out," Quinn said.

"Hopefully," Sam agreed. "I did make progress in a parallel case."

"Parallel case?" Quinn asked.

"I finally managed to track down the girl Denver knew as Cherry."

"Track her down?" I asked. "Is she alive?"

He nodded. "Cherry is now going by another name. She's alive and well and living in Hawaii."

"You spoke to her?" I asked.

He nodded. "Apparently, she left Shipwreck Island of her own free will ten years ago."

"So, she wasn't kidnapped?" I clarified.

He shook his head. "After she won the surfing competition, she headed to Huntington Beach as she told Denver she'd planned to do. When she arrived, she ran into a guy she'd met in the past, and they ended up making a connection of the romantic kind. He was headed to Hawaii, so she followed him and has been living there ever since."

"So, if nothing happened to her, why didn't she show up for her date with Denver?" Carrie asked.

"Actually, I did ask her that, and she said the kid was much too intense and felt like it was better to bail without a big tearful goodbye. Tearful on his part, not on hers," he emphasized.

I had to admit that there was a part of me that really didn't blame her. Denver did tend to be the sort to wear his heart on his sleeve when it came to those he cared about. "So if Cherry simply left the island after the surf competition, then she isn't part of the pattern, which means we still don't have a girl for two thousand and ten," I pointed out.

"That looks to be the case." Sam looked at his watch. "I really need to go. If you hear from Carl, please call me."

"I will," Carrie promised.

"Call me later," Quinn called after Sam. "When you have time to talk."

His expression relaxed, and he sent her the sweetest smile. "I will. Maybe we can even get together later for dinner or a drink or something."

"I'd like that." She smiled back.

After Sam left, the three of us settled onto the deck with tall glasses of iced tea. We still needed to wait for the furniture delivery team, but somehow the idea of emptying boxes while we waited no longer had the appeal it once had. I could see that Carrie was really upset about the situation with Carl. Not that I blamed her. He might be a pig in men's clothing, but he was still the man she'd spent the majority of her life married to.

"So I heard from my friend with Naval Intelligence," Quinn said, I suspected more as a way to initiate a conversation not involving Carl than anything else. "He warned me that the island's perimeter is protected by a laser type security system."

"So even if we're able to land on the island from the backside, we may not be able to make it past the beach," I said.

"Basically, yeah," Quinn responded. "I chatted with my friend, and he did some additional research. Apparently, if we approach at high tide, there is a way to swim beneath the laser fence as long as we approach the island in one specific location. I checked the tide tables, and we do have a couple of opportunities this week. We still need to pick a night when it's extra dark, so ideally, we'll be looking for a foggy or overcast night where the high tide arrives at some point between ten p.m. and four a.m."

"Is there such a night?" Carrie asked.

"Actually," Quinn answered, "if the fog cooperates, we are good to go tomorrow night. High tide is at eleven-fourteen. That should give us time to sneak under the laser fence, take a quick look around, and then swim back out under the fence before the tide starts to go out."

"And is there supposed to be fog all night?" Carrie asked.

"Actually, tomorrow's marine forecast is calling for fog between eight p.m. and four a.m. It should clear by sunrise, but if we're lucky, we should have both the tide and the fog cover we need."

"Are you sure there aren't other security measures in place once you sneak in under the fence?" Carrie asked.

"Honestly?" Quinn answered. "I'm not sure. There's no way to really be sure, but at this point, it seems all we can do is head out to the island and see what we find. We won't have long on the island. Maybe half an hour tops if we want to be safe. We might be able to squeeze out a few more minutes, but if we wait too long and the tide rolls out too far, we'll be trapped until the next high tide."

"It seems pretty risky," Carrie said.

I pursed my lips as I went over the plan in my head. "I don't disagree that it sounds like a risky plan, but I think taking a look around seems to be our best bet of figuring out if Grace is being held there." I glanced at Quinn. "Thirty minutes isn't a lot of time. The island is much too large to explore without at least four times that amount of time."

"I'm aware of that," Quinn answered. "My plan at this point is to access the island and get a general layout of the place. Hopefully, we will be able to ascertain what sort of security we'll need to deal with in the future."

"Future?" Carrie asked.

"My plan is to use tomorrow as a recon mission, which will provide the information we need to sneak back on and stay longer."

"Stay longer?" Carrie's voice rose an octave.

"If we can find a place to hide, then maybe we can sneak onto the island, take a look around, then wait for the next high tide to sneak away," Quinn said.

"Chances are we'd have to be on the island close to twenty-four hours in order to have two high tides under the cover of darkness," I pointed out. "At least at this time of the year when the nights are short."

"Yeah," Quinn sighed. "I did think of that. And I realize that we may have to wait quite a while for the tides and weather to team up in our favor again. But it still seems like a reasonable plan to me to head out tomorrow night and at least check it out if the fog does indeed roll in."

"I'm in," I said.

Carrie blew out a slow breath. "Yeah, okay, I'm in as well. I'll call down to the marina and see about renting a boat. Carl got ours in the divorce settlement."

"Okay, great," Quinn leaned back in her chair with a look of satisfaction on her face. I was scared half out of my mind, but she looked like the cat who'd managed to tip over the carton of cream.

Chapter 4

Shortly after the sun set the following evening, the fog crawled toward the east, enveloping the area as it made its way toward the California coastline. It would remain to be seen if Montgomery Island would be shrouded in fog as we hoped, but according to the marine forecast, the fogbank was a large one, extending nearly fifty miles in each direction. Quinn, Carrie, and I had loaded up the boat we'd rented with the supplies we'd need earlier in the day. It was our plan to head out of the marina an hour or so before sunset. To the casual observer, we hoped it would appear as if our plan for the evening was a sunset dinner cruise, which in these parts was a popular way to bid farewell to another day.

Of course, the reality was that no one would probably have paid a bit of attention to three women leaving the island on a boat even if we hadn't come up with the cover of a sunset cruise. I guessed we'd been talking about our plan long enough that Carrie and I had had time to overthink things.

"Are you sure about this?" Carrie asked as the three of us sat offshore of Montgomery Island, waiting for the tide to come in. "It's not too late to back out."

"We're sure," Quinn answered with conviction. "All we need you to do is to wait with the boat. The fog is thick, so you won't be able to see us once we enter the water, and the cell service on the island may be blocked, so we might not be able to check in, but we shouldn't be gone more than ninety minutes."

"I can't help but worry about guards or dogs. Or both," Carrie said.

"It will be fine," Quinn responded, starting the engine and moving forward.

Based on the tide tables, the high tide would occur within half an hour, so it was time to make our move and slowly approach. I could sense Carrie's panic, so I took her hand in mine and gave it a squeeze. I had to admit that I was a lot more frightened and a lot less certain about our plan than Quinn was, but I'd gone over things numerous times in my mind, assigning variables to every possible scenario I could come up with, and, in the end, I'd decided that the potential reward was worth the risk. It wasn't as if we were trying to penetrate the house. All we planned to do was sneak onto the island from the backside, make our way to the greenhouse, and look inside. While I was certain the house, as well as the buildings located on the west side of Montgomery Island, were well guarded, chances were that the greenhouse and fields on the east side of the island were not.

After ten minutes of moving steadily into the fog, Quinn slowed the boat. "It's starting to get shallow. According to the maps I was able to obtain, the closer to the shore we travel, the rockier it will get. I estimated that we'd need to anchor about a quarter of a mile out and swim in from there."

"Swim?" Carrie said. "I thought you were going to paddle."

"We were until we found out about the laser fence. According to my contact, the laser fence is designed to sound an alarm if the laser is broken. This particular fence, however, cannot penetrate water, so the plan is to swim in under the laser at high tide when the water breaks the lowest laser ray in one spot, look around, and then swim back out, using the same low spot we accessed on the way in. If we bring the boards, there's no guarantee we'll have anywhere to leave them once we arrive at the fence."

Carrie's look of worry turned to panic. "Are you really sure about this? It sounds dangerous."

"I'm sure," Quinn said. She looked at me. "How about it? Are you up for this?"

I swallowed hard and nodded. A quarter of a mile was an easy swim. Not that I'd spent a lot of time in the water lately, but I was a strong swimmer, and the water was relatively calm tonight. "I'm sure." I looked at Carrie. "Quinn and I have on full wetsuits. They will provide floatation, and we're both strong swimmers."

After moving forward at a crawl for half a mile or so, Quinn cut the engine and dropped anchor. She glanced into the thick fog and then looked at her watch. "We should get ready."

We'd brought wet suits, fins, and diving packs that we'd filled with portable air canisters in the event we got into trouble, a waterproof camera, binoculars, and a dive computer. We'd synched the dive watches to the dive computer, which would allow us to not only keep track of the time but would also provide GPS data so we'd end up where we intended and weren't thrown off course.

Once we were suited up, Quinn and I slipped into the inky black water.

"We just need to swim about a quarter of a mile straight ahead," Quinn said to me. "The fog is thick, but not so thick as to limit immediate visibility. Just stay behind me. Keep your eyes on my fins. We'll be fine."

"Okay," I said. "I'm ready."

As Quinn and I swam steadily toward the shore, I had to wonder if Quinn really did do stuff like this all the time. She didn't seem frightened. In fact, she seemed energized. I supposed on some level, I shared the rush that came from being part of a covert operation with her, but part of me was terrified. Of course, when I'd been with the FBI, I was a behind the scenes sort of operative while she was used to being on the front lines.

The swim to the shoreline didn't take long. When we arrived at the shallow water that bordered the island, we paused to locate the fence which really only appeared as a row of posts since the lasers weren't visible to the naked eye and the low lying channel Quinn's contact had told us about.

"There," Quinn pointed after she'd taken a few minutes to study the shoreline. "We need to swim under the fence there."

I looked toward a channel that had filled with the tide. I supposed I had to take it on faith that the fence was even on and that swimming beneath the water as we accessed the island would prevent the alarm from sounding. I supposed I was also taking it on faith that there weren't additional alarms or traps set up that we didn't know about.

"Be sure to swim beneath the waterline as you cross the fence line," Quinn warned. Move your pack around to the front so it won't accidentally trip the alarm."

"Okay," I said.

"I'll go first. Stay close behind, and whatever you do, don't surface until you are in the clear."

I took a deep breath and nodded. Quinn dipped down beneath the surface of the water. I followed. When I was a teen, I swam almost every day during the summer, but as an adult, I rarely found my way into the water. I just hoped I'd be able to hold my breath long enough to make it under the fence safely.

The deepwater channel was dark and narrow, which only served to ignite every instinct I had to surface, but eventually, the water shallowed, and Quinn crawled out onto the shoreline. I followed.

"We made it," I said, breathing heavily.

"Was there ever any doubt we would?" Quinn asked.

"Honestly, yes."

Quinn looked at her watch. "We need to be back here in twenty minutes. Leave the fins and the packs here. We'll take the camera and binoculars with us."

I slipped off my fins as well as my hood. I grabbed the supplies we'd need and followed Quinn as she made her way in the direction of the greenhouse. Part of me was amazed that we'd made it this far without sounding an alarm. At least I assumed we'd made it without sounding an alarm. The reality was that there might be a silent alarm that sent security in our direction the minute we'd traversed the fence line.

As we neared the greenhouse, the structure came into view. The fog made it difficult to make out specifics, but it wasn't so thick that it completely hid the shape of the building. Quinn and I made our way around to the door, which surprisingly was open. There were lights on inside the building, which made it risky to enter, but we'd come this far, and the only way I could see to check for Kadupul flowers and opium poppies was to go inside and look around.

"If someone comes along, they'll see us through the windows," I said to Quinn.

"Yeah," she breathed. "This isn't the best setup for a stealthy look around. The fog will make it difficult to see from much of a distance, but if someone does approach, we're toast." She looked around the room. "The raised beds will provide some degree of protection. Stoop down and stay low as we search the place row by row. We know what we're looking for, which should make the search a quick one."

"Even if we find both of these flowers in this greenhouse, do you think the presence of the flowers will be enough for Sam to get a search warrant?"

"I don't know. Maybe. The Kadupul flower is pretty rare in these parts. I suppose that Sam can use that detail to demonstrate that there is a good likelihood that Veronica Smith was here before she died. The fact that she drowned under mysterious circumstances might get him the warrant he needs to take a closer look around."

"I hope so. If not, I'm not sure what our next move would be."

Quinn looked at her watch. "We're running out of time. Let's split up. You take the three rows along the back, and I'll take the next three rows. Meet me outside when you're done. And hurry. If we miss our high tide window, we'll be stuck on this island until the next high tide."

"Okay," I stepped up the pace, moving as quickly as I could, given the need to crouch down and stay low. After Quinn and I split up, things moved along quickly, and I managed to confirm that the rows I searched contained neither flower we were looking for. I hoped Quinn had been more successful. I paused as I made my way toward the door, looking around one more time. The greenhouse contained a lot of interesting plants, but none seemed to be the sort to provide food or serve as a cash crop. I wondered why Gavin Montgomery even bothered.

As I slipped out of the greenhouse into the darkness, I could hear voices coming in our direction. I stuck my head back inside. "Someone's coming," I said, probably louder than I should have.

Quinn headed toward the door and slipped outside just as the image of two people walking toward us penetrated the fog.

"Is anyone there?" the voice of a woman called out.

I could hear Quinn breathing as we crouched behind a tree that was barely large enough to hide one person, let alone two. I held my breath as one of the women stepped toward us. She appeared to look right at me before she turned back toward her friend.

"No one's here," the woman who I was certain had seen me said to her friend. "You know how voices carry out here. The voices you heard were probably coming from staff housing. Let's just get what we need and get back. It creeps me out to be walking around with the fog so thick."

The woman who seemed to be covering for us for some reason stepped into the well-lit building, providing a clear view through the window. Quinn put her hand over my mouth at the exact moment I let out an involuntary gasp. After a few seconds, I nodded to let her know it was okay to remove her hand. Quinn lifted her camera and took a photo.

Oh my God, I mouthed, although I didn't utter a sound.

Quinn squeezed my hand as the women completed their task and then left.

"We need to go," Quinn said as soon as the women disappeared from sight.

"But…"

"Now," she added, grabbing my hand. "Our window to make it under the fence is waning, so run."

I did as Quinn said, and ran as fast as I could, given the fact that I was still wearing a full-length wetsuit and my feet were bare other than the booties that came with the wetsuit. When we arrived at the spot where we needed to swim out, I could see that the water was receding quickly. I grabbed my fins, hood, and backpack and entered the water. I could hear Quinn behind me as I struggled to stay low enough to avoid the laser now that the water was not nearly as deep as it had been. In the end, I had to pull myself through with my hands rather than risk kicking my legs. It wasn't until I was well clear of the fence that I paused and allowed myself to catch my breath.

"Was that Peggy?" I was finally able to voice once Quinn emerged behind me, and we were both treading water while we pulled on our hoods and fins for the swim back.

"It looked like her, but keep in mind that it's been twenty-five years, and we didn't get a good look at either woman."

"She saw me," I said. "I know she did. She looked right at me, but instead of sounding the alarm, she covered for us with her friend."

"I know. I saw her, as well. But there are other reasons for the woman to have covered for us. We can't just assume, based on a quick glance, that the woman we saw was our missing friend."

"But you got a photo," I stated.

"I did," she confirmed. She lowered her leg after positioning her fins. "Now, let's get out of here. I'm sure Carrie is frantic by now."

The swim back out to the boat was a lot less tense for me than the swim to the island, although I had to admit my mind was racing. Could the woman we saw actually have been the friend I was certain had been dead for all these years? She hadn't appeared to be under any sort of duress. In fact, she looked healthy and happy. Of course, if she had been trapped on the island for all this time, then it did make sense that she would have found a way to make the best of it.

"I've been so worried," Carrie called over the side of the boat as Quinn slipped off her fins and handed them up to her.

"It took a little longer than we hoped, but we made it through fine," Quinn replied as she climbed the ladder.

I slipped off my fins, passed them up, and then followed Quinn up the ladder.

"So did you find the flowers you need to prove Veronica was on the island?" Carrie asked.

I glanced at Quinn. We'd never compared notes.

"I didn't," Quinn said.

"Me either," I seconded.

"So, what does that mean?" Carrie asked as Quinn began raising the anchor.

"It means that unless there's a second greenhouse somewhere, Veronica probably wasn't on Montgomery Island before she died," I said. "That doesn't mean she was never there, but she sure as heck didn't pick up the flower petal or the seeds from that greenhouse."

"So, the mission was a bust?" Carrie asked.

"Not necessarily," I said. "Just as Quinn and I were finishing up, two women arrived. I swear one of them looked like Peggy."

Carrie's eyes widened. "Peggy? Are you sure?"

"Actually, no," I said. "I only got a glimpse of the woman, and a lot of time has passed. Peggy, had she lived, would be forty-one now, and this woman looked to be around that same age. She had blond hair, and her features were similar to Peggy's, but I really can't say for certain. Quinn got a photo. Maybe once we take a second look, we'll be able to decide one way or the other."

"If Peggy has been on that island all these years, doesn't it seem like she would have found a way off by now?" Carrie asked.

I lifted a shoulder. "It's not an easy place to gain access to if you are uninvited, and I imagine it wouldn't be an easy place to leave if the person who took you there doesn't want you to leave. I guess at this point, all we can do is plead our case and hope that Sam can get a warrant, and can take a look around and get our answers once and for all.

Chapter 5

I wasn't sure I was going to be able to pull myself out of bed in time to make my morning run with Ryder after staying up most of the night with Carrie and Quinn, discussing the woman we'd seen on the island, so I texted him before drifting off to sleep to let him know that I'd stayed up late with Carrie and Quinn and would probably just sleep in. He texted back and let me know that he would probably just go into work early. He also asked if I wanted to get together for lunch, providing, of course, that he didn't have an emergency of some sort to deal with. I told him I'd call him later.

Of course, in the end, I didn't end up sleeping nearly as long as I'd hoped to. The idea that the woman on the island could be Peggy had left my head spinning.

After we'd gotten home, Quinn had downloaded the photo she'd taken to the computer. The image had been captured through a window, and the angle of the shot only provided a profile view. It was to be expected that a forty-one-year-old woman would look a lot different than her sixteen-year-old self, but there were small things that brought Peggy to mind when we considered the image on the computer screen. In the end, we couldn't decide if the woman in the photo was Peggy, or if she was simply someone who shared similar physical characteristics with Peggy, but it did appear that the woman had seen Quinn and me hiding behind the tree and let us go. If not Peggy, then who? I figured the best thing to do at this point was to fill Sam in, which I intended to do once I was able to contact him and make an appointment for us to get together.

"Morning," Quinn said, joining me on the deck where I'd settled in with a mug of coffee. "I didn't expect anyone else to be up yet." She glanced at her phone. "We just went to bed about four hours ago."

"I couldn't sleep," I said. "I'm sure I'll be tired later, but right now, I actually feel pretty wound up."

Quinn tucked her legs up under her body as she settled into one of the patio chairs. "Yeah, me too. Besides, I'm used to sleeping in spurts if there's something going on." She took a sip of her coffee. "It's a gorgeous day. Might even be a good day to go surfing."

While I appreciated the fact that Quinn seemed to be adept at compartmentalizing, it wasn't a skill I was quite as proficient at. "Actually, I've been sitting out here thinking we need to tell Sam what we know. We didn't want to involve him until we knew something, but now that we have something to share, I think we should share it."

Quinn sipped from her mug again before answering. "I guess we can call him, or we can simply head into town and see if he's in his office."

"Let's text him and let him know we want to talk to him. That way, we won't waste a trip. I told Ryder I'd meet him for lunch, but it's only eight o'clock now, so maybe we can meet Sam in an hour or two."

Quinn picked her phone up off the table. "I'll text him."

Sam texted Quinn back right away, letting her know that he was planning to head into town about nine. We arranged to meet him in his office at nine-thirty, which gave me time to have a second cup of coffee, shower, and dress for the day.

"Do you think he's going to be mad?" I asked Quinn after she confirmed a time with Sam.

She shrugged. "I don't know. Maybe. But I'm not sure Sammy being mad or not is really the point of any of this. If there is one thing I learned a long time ago, it's that you do what you need to do and let other people worry about how they want to react."

"So, you never worry about making others mad when you're after a story?" I asked. "You never worry about hurting them or worrying them or even doing something that might do permanent damage to your relationship?"

"Nope." She set her mug on the table and stretched her arms over her head. "As a reporter after the truth, I can't worry about any of that. I have a job to do, and I do it. End of story."

Wow. I knew Quinn had a hard side, but I guess I never realized how hard it might actually be.

"What about people you know and care about?" I asked. "If you found something out about me that would hurt me deeply if that fact was made public, would you print it anyway if instructed to?"

She hesitated. "That's not a real situation, so it doesn't make sense to spend time analyzing it. All I can say at this point is maybe."

"Maybe?" I asked.

She shifted in her chair, settling one foot on the ground, but keeping the other leg tucked up under her body. "I don't mess around with minor news stories or unsubstantiated leads, so theoretically, if I had been investigating your secret, then it stands to reason that your secret must be a pretty big deal." She adjusted her position just a bit. "It's not like I write for a gossip rag. I write hard-hitting exposés about very real crisis in the world," she reminded me. "If, in the course, of my search for the truth, I found out that someone I knew and loved was somehow involved in something newsworthy, and if not exposing their involvement might lead to innocent people being harmed in some way, then yes, I would expose your secret even if it caused you harm. But that's unlikely to ever occur unless you're actually a double agent or undercover operative, so it isn't a scenario I really need to worry about."

"So, you're not at all worried that Sam will be hurt that we went sneaking around behind his back?"

She shrugged. "I suppose I would be lying if I said I didn't care if he was hurt, but we knew when we came up with the plan that he might be hurt or angry, and we did it anyway. Ryder, too, for that matter. At this point, worrying about something happening that we knew from the beginning could very well happen seems like a waste of energy."

I supposed Quinn had a point. We did know from the beginning that both Sam and Ryder might be upset that we'd left them out of the plan. I supposed all we could do at this point was live with any fallout caused by our decision.

Carrie still hadn't come down from her suite by the time Quinn and I needed to leave to meet Sam, so we left her a note. It was probably best that she stay out of this anyway. Neither Quinn nor I lived on the island, so if our action caused friction with Sam, that discomfort would only last a few more weeks. Carrie, on the other hand, lived here full-time and had to face the man on a regular basis.

"Is your life always this stressful?" I asked Quinn as I drove toward Sam's office.

She laughed. "This is nothing. The degree of stress I normally live with on a daily basis makes our little outing last night seem like a cakewalk."

"Do you ever tire of the constant pressure?"

Quinn shrugged. "Sometimes. I told you when I came to the island that I was burnt out and ready for a break. And I was. In fact, I still am. I know my boss is confused about my unwillingness to take a break from the vacation I requested to do these little jobs for him, but I really feel that I need to completely step away for a while."

"I don't blame you." I pulled into a parking spot next to the sheriff's office. "What you do is very demanding. Most people would have burnt out long before this."

Quinn opened her door and stepped out. I stepped out of the driver's side onto the street. "So, how should we handle this?" I asked.

"I guess we just jump in and see where we end up," Quinn said, heading toward the front door.

"Morning, Sam," I said after entering the room.

"Kelly; Quinn," he greeted. "I'm surprised the two of you are out and about so early. Is something going on?"

"We're just looking for an update on the investigation," Quinn said to Sam after he'd offered us seats in the conference room.

"Is that why you wanted to meet? To get an update?" Sam asked. "When you texted, you indicated that you had something to share."

"We do," Quinn answered. "But I figured we'd get an update from you first."

He frowned. "Okay. I do have news. Several things, in fact."

"We're all ears," Quinn said.

"First of all, I was finally able to track down Carl. It turns out he's in Portland this week and hasn't been monitoring his cell as often as he usually does. He confirmed that Grace had called him on Saturday night to ask about a house he has listed for sale on the island, which belongs to a man named Rain Spivey."

"That name is familiar," I said.

"Rain is a musician," Quinn provided. "He's actually a pretty big deal with the under thirty crowd."

"Okay, so Grace called Carl to find out about a house Rain is selling. Why?" I said.

"Carl told me that Grace told him that she had a friend who was interested in looking at it if it was still available. He explained that he was out of town and wouldn't be able to show it until he returned. Grace asked for the address. She said the friend wanted to drive by it. He gave her the address as well as the phone number of a woman who works in his office. Carl said he told Grace that the house was unoccupied, so it would be okay if they wanted to look in the windows, but if her friend wanted to go inside, he should call his colleague. I called the woman whose number was given to Grace by Carl, but she said that Grace never called."

"That's weird, right?" I asked. "Why would a sixteen-year-old girl be calling about a house for sale on the island? If Grace actually did have a friend who was interested in the house, why wouldn't the friend just call?"

"I thought the same thing," Sam said. "I asked the woman Carl had referred Grace to to meet me at the house. She agreed to do so, and we looked around. We found a broken window at the back of the property, and the security system had been disabled remotely. It seemed obvious that someone had broken in. I had the guys from the county dust the place, and was able to determine that Grace and at least two other people were in the house at some point."

"But you don't know who she was with or why they broke in?" I asked.

"Not yet. According to the Realtor I spoke to, nothing obvious seems to be missing, but she didn't have a complete inventory and planned to call Rain. The guys from the county office are still running the prints. Nothing popped right off, but I'm still hopeful we'll be able to identify the individuals with Grace."

"Why would Grace run away from home and then help someone break into a vacant house?" I asked.

Sam blew out a breath. "I don't know. I figure either they must have been looking for something specific, or they just thought it would be a rush to hang out in the home of someone famous. I don't know why Grace did what she did, and I hope her taking off is a result of teenage rebellion, but given the fact that the security system was disabled, I sort of doubt a group of teens is behind the break-in."

"I don't know, there are some pretty tech-savvy teens out there these days," Quinn pointed out.

"Maybe," Sam agreed. "Whomever Grace is with, I just hope she is hanging out with them voluntarily."

"So, do you think she might have been forced to call Carl about the house?" Quinn asked.

"I think that's a possibility," Sam answered. "If Grace simply needed a place to cool down after her fight with her mother, why not just go to a friend's house? Breaking into a vacant house seems like a drastic step to take."

"So if Grace left the party on Saturday night to help someone, who has yet to be identified, break into this house, where is she now?" I asked. "It's been four days. That's a long time to hang onto a grudge, no matter how mad she'd been at her mother."

"I wish I knew the answer to that," Sam said.

"Anything else?" Quinn asked. "Either about Grace or one of the other missing girls?"

I couldn't tell if Quinn was really interested or if she was stalling. Maybe she was more nervous about Sam being angry with us than she would admit.

"About Grace, no," Sam answered. "But I did receive a lead yesterday relating to the disappearance of Veronica Smith. That lead took me north, almost to the Oregon border. That's the reason I couldn't get together with you yesterday."

"I remember you said you had to go out of town for the day. What'd you find?" Quinn asked.

"I found out where Veronica has been up until a few days before drowning in the ocean, and I found the greenhouse that produces both the Kadupul flower and opium poppies."

My eyes widened. "You did. Where?"

"The greenhouse where Veronica seems to have picked up both the petal from the Kadupul flower and the seeds from the opium poppies is located on a commune north of here. The property is pretty remote, with only a single dirt road accessing the small commune, which isn't even featured on the map I was working from. I drove up to the community yesterday and spoke to a man who lives on the commune. He confirmed that Veronica had spent time on the property, although she did tend to come and go. Apparently, she showed up five years ago with a man named Indigo. According to Kai, the man I spoke to, Indigo had been an occasional resident of the commune and asked for permission for him and Veronica to stay. Kai said it appeared that Veronica was desperate for a place to hide out, so permission was conditionally granted."

"Conditionally?" Quinn asked.

"It seems that the structure under which the commune operates is pretty rigid," Sam explained. "There are rules that must be adhered to. If you don't adhere, you're out. Kai told me that a year or so after Veronica arrived, she decided she didn't want to follow so many rules, so she left. She came back for a short stay about a year after that and then left again. Most recently, she showed up about six months ago, but when it became apparent that she was not willing to do her part, the council kicked her out. They gave her a week to vacate the property. On the third day of her seven-day grace period, she snuck out in the middle of the night with plants from the greenhouse. Initially, Kai was reluctant to specify what sort of plants she took off with, but I was finally able to determine that the plants she stole were opium poppies."

"Isn't it illegal to grow opium poppies?" I asked.

"It is," Sam verified. "But this group is a peaceful group that doesn't cause any problems and is mostly left alone by local law enforcement. The poppies are utilized by the group for spiritual ceremonies, and I've been assured they are not sold for use on the street. Of course, having said that, they do have value, and I imagine Veronica realized that."

"So Veronica is kicked off the commune and needs cash to settle somewhere else, so she steals the poppies with the intent of selling them?" Quinn asked.

"That's my guess," Sam said.

"So how did she end up dead on the beach?" I asked.

"I don't know for certain, but I'm going to speculate that her deal went bad, and she either voluntarily jumped from a boat with the hope of escaping, or she was pushed. I don't know who she met or where she went, but Kai did say that Veronica was last seen on Saturday evening, and we know she was found dead on the beach on Tuesday morning. Where she was between the two pinpoints is anyone's guess."

"What if she was killed by someone from the commune?" I asked. "When the plants turned up missing the same day that Veronica left, they must have figured out that she was the one who took them. What if someone from the commune tracked her down and killed her?"

"I suppose that is a possibility," Sam answered. "I'm afraid we're in the same situation as we are with the Montgomery estate. Without a warrant, my hands are tied, and without a compelling reason to link Veronica's death with a commune more than a hundred miles away, I'll never find a judge to issue a warrant. So what's the interesting news you have to share?"

I froze. I looked at Quinn. She nodded toward me and then began to speak. "Kelly and I thought, wrongly as it turns out, that the petal from the Kadupul flower and the seeds from the opium poppy had come from a greenhouse we knew existed on Montgomery Island based on aerial shots I managed to obtain. We knew that the island was impenetrable without an invite, and we also knew that you were never going to get an invite without a warrant, a warrant we all know would only be forthcoming with some sort of evidence to indicate that Grace and perhaps the other missing girls were being kept there."

He raised a brow. It did sound as if the very articulate Quinn was rambling.

"Quinn and I found a way to sneak onto the island for a quick peek, and we took it," I jumped in.

"What!" Sam spat.

"Don't worry, we had a plan," Quinn jumped back in. "A good plan. All we wanted to do was prove that the two flowers in question existed on the island."

"They didn't," I added.

"Of course, we didn't know about your lead up north," Quinn said, looking a bit more shaken than I was used to seeing her. "We didn't know that you'd already solved that part of the puzzle." She paused. "We knew it would be illegal for you to access the island without permission, so we decided to leave you out of it."

"It was illegal for the two of you to access the island without permission as well," Sam pointed out. "It's called trespassing."

"We were only on the island for twenty minutes, and no one knows we were there," I assured Sam, realizing that the woman who saw us did know we were there.

"How did you manage to access the island that is famous for being inaccessible without an invite?" he asked.

Quinn explained about the fence and the high tide loophole.

Sam paled visibly. "You could have been shot."

"We could have been, but we weren't," Quinn argued.

"Maybe not, but you took a huge risk, and, as it turns out, that risk was for nothing."

"Not nothing," I countered Sam's statement. "We think Peggy might be on the island." I took the photo we'd printed out of my purse.

Sam took the photo, his frown deepening as he looked at it. "You took this photo on the island?"

I nodded. "Just last night. It does look like her. Right?"

He furrowed his brow as he studied the image. "It looks like it could be her." He walked out of the room. I looked at Quinn. She shrugged. He walked in a few minutes later with a file in his hand. He opened a file and set several photos of sixteen-year-old Peggy on the table. He then set the photo Quinn had taken next to them for comparison.

"Look at this little mole on the right side of Peggy's upper lip," Quinn pointed. "This woman has that same little mole."

Chapter 6

I honestly thought it would take Sam days to gain access to the island, but as it turned out, he simply called Wilson and asked to speak to him about a girl who'd been missing for the past twenty-five years, and amazingly, Wilson agreed to allow not only Sam to access the island but Quinn and me as well. I felt bad leaving Carrie out of things, but Wilson hadn't included her in the invite, and I didn't want to muck up the works by trying to have her added to the guest list after permission had already been granted.

When we arrived at the island's private dock, we were met by an armed guard. He checked our ID's and then led us to a room that was located in one of the long buildings behind the main house. We were told to wait and that someone would be with us shortly.

"This Gavin Montgomery guy runs this island like a small country," Quinn said. "Very impressive."

"Impressive or creepy?" I asked.

She lifted a shoulder. "Maybe a bit of both."

"I wonder if Gavin Montgomery knows we're here?" I asked.

"I'm sure he does," Sam replied. "I would be willing to bet that nothing goes on that he doesn't know about."

I supposed Sam was right. Not that he'd make an appearance. Based on what I'd heard, no one other than Wilson and a few select staff had access to the reclusive billionaire.

About fifteen minutes after we were shown to the room, the door opened, and Peggy walked in.

"Peggy?" I asked.

She nodded, tears streaming down her face.

"Oh my God," I said as I crossed the room and wrapped her in a hug. "I can't believe it's really you. I thought you were dead. We all thought you were dead."

"I know," she cried into my shoulder. "I'm so sorry. So very, very sorry."

I glanced over Peggy's shoulder to find Quinn frowning at her. "Very sorry for what?" Quinn asked in a tone that seemed to lack warmth.

Peggy pulled back from me. She looked at Quinn. "Hi, Quinn."

"Sorry for what?" Quinn asked again.

Peggy took a deep breath. "I guess we should talk." She looked at Sam. "It's fine if you stay, but the reason I asked Wilson to allow you on the island was so I could have a chance to explain things to my friends. Your invite does not extend beyond this room."

"I understand," he said. "I just need to ask you one question, and I need you to answer honestly."

"Okay."

"Are you currently being, or have you ever been, held here against your will?"

"No." Peggy indicated that we should all sit down. I was so happy to see her that I didn't want to let go of her, so I sat down next to her, clinging to her hand all the while. Quinn and Sam both looked less than thrilled, which I didn't really understand. Peggy was alive. They should be turning cartwheels, not staring at her like she was somehow the bad guy.

"So, what happened?" I asked, "Why are you here?"

She took a deep breath as tears streamed down her face. "I need to tell you something that I've only shared with a few people. It isn't easy for me to talk about, so just let me get through it without saying anything."

We all agreed to Peggy's request.

She took a deep breath, squeezing the hand I still held. It seemed to me that she was working up the courage to speak. Whatever was going on, it must be bad.

"When I turned fourteen, my dad molested me," she choked out.

I gasped, but Quinn and Sam didn't even look surprised.

Peggy continued. "At that point, it was just the one time, he apologized, and I was so ashamed that I didn't tell anyone. Then when I turned fifteen, he did it again, only this time he seemed less apologetic. He tried to tell me that it was natural, that he loved me, and that a lot of fathers were intimate with their daughters. I knew it wasn't true, but I was scared and ashamed and didn't know what to do. By the time my family came to the island that summer, the frequency of the visits from my father had increased. I wanted to stop them, but I didn't know how to accomplish that. Eventually, I realized I'd had enough, so I told my mother what was going on." Peggy swiped angrily at the tears that she couldn't seem to control. "I was so scared to talk to her, but I'd met Dusty that summer, and we'd become friends, and he convinced me that I should come clean with my mother, so I worked up my courage and told her everything."

So maybe Dusty had been a friend and not a skeezy lover as I'd thought. Or maybe the reason she'd confided in him was because he was a lover. I supposed we could sort that out later, not that it really mattered at this point.

"And?" Quinn asked, seeming to forget her promise to let Peggy finish before speaking.

"And nothing." Peggy took a breath. "When I told my mother what my father had been doing to me, I expected her to be shocked. I expected her to help me. But instead, she told me that she knew what had been going on. She told me that my father was sick and had some issues to deal with, but that he was getting help. She begged me not to tell. She said if my dad was arrested, we'd lose everything. Both houses, our cars, our cash. I was so hurt and so angry, but at least my dad wasn't around much that summer, so I figured I had time to think about things. But then he came to the island for a weekend, and it happened again. I knew my mom wouldn't help, so I called my brother. When he showed up, I thought he was going to help me, but when he arrived, he told me that the dream job he was set to move right into after graduating college was being provided to him as a favor to Dad by one of Dad's friends. He, like my mother, begged me to keep things to myself. I guess I sort of lost it at that point. I was scared and alone and didn't know what to do, so I did the only thing I could think of, I started planning to run away."

"You could have come to us," I said.

"I couldn't," she said so softly that I could barely make out what she was staying. "It was just too awful. Too embarrassing. I didn't want you to know. Any of you."

"So how did you end up here?" Sam eventually asked.

She swallowed and then took in a long slow breath, which she blew out just as slowly. Once she'd regained her composure, she began to speak. "I'd met Wilson that summer. He was sort of a dork, but he was easy to talk to, and we became friends. I'm not even sure why I told him my secret. I'd never told anyone other than Dusty, my mother, and brother, but shortly after my dad had been on the island for a few days and then had gone home, I came across Wilson sitting alone on the beach. He was drinking tequila, and he offered me some. I was beyond upset, so I accepted even though I barely knew the guy. Somewhere that night, when I arrived at that critical point between being totally drunk and passing out, I spilled my secret. When I came to the next day, he offered me an out. He told me I could sneak away and come to his island with him. He assured me that no one would find me here. I wasn't sure at first, but he said the offer was open and that I could take some time to think about it. We started hanging out, and I began to trust him. I really thought I'd turn him down in the end, but then my brother told me that my dad planned another visit, and I panicked. I ran into

Wilson at the surf competition, told him that I'd thought about it, and was ready to leave. We met up that night."

"And you've been here all this time?" I asked.

She nodded.

"We were all so scared and so worried when you disappeared," Quinn said. "Why didn't you tell anyone what you were doing?"

"My father was a powerful attorney with all sorts of political allies. He had friends in law enforcement and friends in the government; friends strategically placed to protect him from prosecution. I knew in my heart that even if I told the police or a teacher or someone what had happened, he'd find a way to twist it around and make it look like I was lying. My own brother and mother were on his side, so I had little reason to believe that anyone would be on mine. I thought about just taking off, but I was afraid the cops would find me and make me go back, so when Wilson gave me an out, I took it. I found a home on the island. I'm safe here."

"So are you and Wilson a couple?" I asked.

"No. We're just friends. Wilson isn't into complicated relationships. He has an agreement with a couple of women on Shipwreck Island, but all his relationships here on this island are platonic."

"So, are there other women who live here on the island?" Sam asked.

"Sure. The island is mostly self-sustaining. It takes people to accomplish that. Everyone who lives here pitches in. I work in the garden, which is how I knew you'd been here."

"You saw us?" Quinn asked.

Peggy nodded. "I didn't say anything at the time since I had a friend with me, and I wasn't sure how to handle it, but I decided to confide in Wilson because I have no reason not to trust him. He was curious as to how someone was able to access the island but didn't seem particularly angry about it. I think the secrecy thing is more his father's deal. Anyway he agreed that if someone called asking about me, he'd allow me to talk to them if I felt I wanted to."

"So, he won't be attending this meeting?" Sam asked.

"No. But he hasn't done anything wrong. I promise you that."

"And the other women are all here of their own free will?" Sam asked.

Peggy nodded. "Any of us can leave at any time. And many do leave. I chose to stay because I'm safe and happy here."

"Is Grace Johnson here?" Sam asked.

Peggy slowly shook her head. "I don't know anyone by that name."

Sam took a photo out of his pocket. "This is a recent photo of her. Do you recognize her?"

Peggy looked at the photo. "No. I really don't."

"How about her?" He showed her a photo of Veronica Smith.

Peggy looked at it closely. "No. I'm sorry. I've never seen her before."

Sam showed her photos of Gina Baldwin and Hillary Denton. "These are old photos, more than a decade old, but do you recognize either of these girls?"

She pointed to Gina. "This one, no, but the other one is Hillary. She was here for a while, but she left after she had her baby."

"Baby?" Sam asked.

Peggy explained. "Hillary came here to get away from a bad situation, much like I did. She was pregnant and a minor. Her parents wanted her to have an abortion, but she said no. They told her that if she had the baby, it would be taken from her before she was even able to hold it. They told her that a baby would ruin her life. Hillary wanted her baby so very badly, so when Wilson offered her sanctuary, she took it. She came to the island and had her baby. She lived here, working with me in the garden until she was eighteen. Once she turned eighteen, she no longer had to fear her parents, so Wilson gave her some money and helped her get started somewhere else."

Sam frowned.

I suspect Peggy noticed this because the next thing she said was said with conviction. "Wilson helped us. Maybe it's illegal to harbor a runaway, but he gave us an alternative when we needed one. If you do anything to try to hurt him, I'll deny saying any of this."

"Sammy isn't here to arrest Wilson for helping you," Quinn said. "Are you Sammy?"

"No," he said. "I guess not. But if I find out that there are any girls on the island who are here against their will, then we have a different story."

"No one is here against their will," Peggy said. "It isn't like that. Besides, if Wilson was holding girls here against their will, do you honestly think he'd have invited you here to talk to me?"

"No, I guess not," Sam admitted.

"Don't make me regret being honest with you," Peggy said. "Wilson probably saved my life. Before he offered me a safe haven, I'd seriously considered suicide as a viable option. I know there are those who consider him odd, but he has a genuine heart. You can trust him."

"I believe you," I said.

Peggy glanced at the clock on the wall. "The guards will be here in a few minutes to escort you back to your boat. I'm glad I was able to explain what happened, but I don't want my dad or brother to know where I am. Promise me you won't tell."

"I won't tell your dad or brother or anyone else," I said. "But Carrie and Nora and Ryder have all been helping us look for all the missing girls, including you. I need to tell them what you told us."

Peggy took in a deep breath and then blew it out slowly. "Okay. But only them. As safe as I feel here, I'm pretty sure that if my father and brother know where I am, I'll never feel safe again."

"Do you think they'd hurt you to prevent you from telling what happened?" Sam asked.

"In a heartbeat. I don't trust either of them, so please promise me. As far as anyone needs to know, other than Carrie, Nora, and Ryder, you never found me, and we never talked."

I promised, but I noticed that neither Sam nor Quinn followed my lead. Lord, I hoped they'd keep Peggy's secret as she'd asked us to.

Chapter 7

"So, what now?" I asked after we'd said our goodbyes to Peggy and had been escorted back to Sam's boat.

Sam turned the key in the ignition and backed the boat out of the slip we'd been shown to when we first arrived. "I suppose, technically, Wilson broke the law when he chose to harbor a minor who'd run away, but given the fact that Peggy disappeared twenty-five years ago and she seems to have come to the island of her own free will, I'm not sure that beating that drum would be worth it. If I find that Grace or other minors are currently living on the island, I'll have no choice but to follow up."

"It seems that if Grace was here on the island, Wilson wouldn't have let us anywhere near the place," Quinn pointed out. "Besides, based on the break-in at Rain's home, it seems like something else going on with her."

"I have to agree with that," Sam said. "It likewise sounds as if Hillary Denton had a good reason to run away if Peggy was correct, and her parents had plans to force her to give the baby she wanted to keep up for adoption. At the time, a lot of her friends actually did report that it was likely she simply took off, and at this point, I'm assuming, like some have speculated, that she left her car at Lover's Point to throw everyone off. I'm not sure I can find her if she doesn't want to be found, but I do think I'll take a look and see what I can find. If she had a baby with her when she left the area and didn't change her name, I might be able to pick up her trail."

"I guess it would be good to know that she really is okay," I said.

"I'd say that at this point, if Peggy and Hillary both ran away, Cherry is alive and living in Hawaii, and Veronica was last seen on a commune in Northern California, your original theory of a five-year pattern of girls going missing by the same person is shot all to hell," Quinn pointed out.

"Yes," Sam agreed. "That has occurred to me as well."

"You look exhausted," I said to Sam after he removed one of his hands from the steering wheel of the boat to rub his eyes.

"It's been a long few days. There seems to be several different things going on, but finding Grace is my number one priority. When I thought all six missing teen cases were related in some way, I figured that if I solved one case, I'd solve them all, but I can see now that is not going to happen."

"So, what are you planning to do next in terms of Grace's missing person case?" Quinn asked.

"I don't know," Sam admitted. "The lead relating to the break-in at Rain's house might lead us to a new clue, but the break-in occurred days ago, so I'm not sure how much help any evidence we still might find at the scene will provide. I'm afraid looking for clues related to six missing persons cases that have turned out not to be related at all, has only served to dilute my efforts to find Grace. I really should have treated her case as an isolated incident from the beginning. I'd probably be further along if I had."

"It's also your job to find out what happened to Veronica Smith," Quinn pointed out. "She did turn up dead on your beach."

"It is my job to find out how she died," Sam admitted. "But she's dead. I can't help her now. Grace, on the other hand, might still be alive and waiting to be rescued."

"I keep thinking about the man who offered Grace a surfing sponsorship," Quinn said. "It was the offer that caused the friction between Grace and Lizzy. What if that was intentional to gain Grace's cooperation? I wonder if Grace ever mentioned his name to Lizzy."

"I asked Lizzy about the man who spoke to Grace," Sam informed us. "She said that Grace told her his name was Ethan. Grace also told her that she couldn't remember his last name, but she did remember that he worked for the Fairchild Agency, which is based in LA. I called the Fairchild Agency, and the woman I spoke to assured me that they did not now, nor have they ever had an agent named Ethan. She also assured me that if one of their agents would have been interested in Grace, none of them would have approached a minor without his or her parent or guardian being present."

"So the guy was a phony," I said.

"That was my take on it. I've spoken to the event organizers, and none admitted to having any knowledge of an agent named Ethan. I also spoke to the surfers who came in second to fifth place, and none had been approached. Lizzy was going to ask around to see if anyone had encountered this Ethan. She's attended the competition every year since her girls were old enough to participate, so she knows all the players."

"As Kelly said, maybe this Ethan used the lure of sponsorship to get Grace to meet him somewhere alone," Quinn said. "If we find him, maybe we'll find her as well."

I hoped that was true, and I hoped we wouldn't be too late to save her, but I had to admit I had a bad feeling about things.

After we got back to Shipwreck Island, Sam made a comment about heading home to get some sleep so he could think straight. Quinn offered to go with him. I wasn't sure how much sleeping would occur under that circumstance, but he seemed happy to have Quinn tag along, so I said my goodbyes and then headed home. I still needed to catch Carrie up on everything that had happened, and after deciding to head to Montgomery Island with Sam, I'd changed my lunch date with Ryder to a dinner date, so I had that to get ready for as well.

As I approached the house, I wondered what exactly I was going to say to Carrie. Would she be angry that she'd missed out on seeing Peggy? I supposed if I'd been the one who'd been left out, I'd be feeling pretty bad about things. Nora wasn't here, so not including her wasn't an issue, but all Carrie had done was have the misfortune to sleep in. When I arrived at the house, I found Carrie with an exceptionally good looking man she introduced as Glen. Glen was a neighbor who'd lived across the street from the house she'd lived in with Carl for almost as long as she and Carl had lived in the neighborhood.

"Glen was nice enough to help me take some of the furniture I needed to clear out of the house to the church auxiliary," Carrie said, referring to the charitable organization that accepted donations and then turned them into cash, which they used in community programs. "An offer of a beer seemed an inadequate thank you, but I'm afraid it's all that I had, so here we are."

"I was happy to help," Glen said. "I'm going to miss having you as a neighbor, but I do understand your need for a new start. It was like that for me after Wilma passed away. I didn't sell the house, but I did paint and change out the furniture."

"I remember," Carrie said. "Carl ended up with the pool table that cluttered up my game room for two years before I finally talked him into getting rid of it."

Glen chuckled. "I had a feeling you weren't real happy when he asked if he could have it. Personally, I never really wanted it. It was Wilma who bought it in the first place. I think she was trying to get back at me for the leather sofa she hated."

"Actually, she didn't hate that sofa. She just wanted to make you think she hated it, so she could use it against you if she needed a bargaining chip."

"Like the labradoodle," he laughed.

"Exactly like the labradoodle," Carrie chuckled.

I wasn't sure if the vibe I was picking up on was accurate, but it seemed there was an underlying intimacy to what was being said. I really didn't get it since the conversation seemed ridiculous. I didn't figure this was the best time to tell Carrie about Peggy, so I made my excuses and headed upstairs to get ready for my date with Ryder. I had to admit that I was nervous about bringing him up to speed on the fact that I'd been busy following leads I'd decided not to share with him ahead of time. I hoped he wouldn't be too angry. What I really needed was a night to simply relax and unwind.

By the time I'd showered and dressed in a pair of white shorts and a sunny summer top, Glen had left. I found Carrie sitting on the deck, sipping a glass of wine.

"Did your friend leave?" I asked, even though, given his absence, I could see he'd left.

"He did."

"He seems like a nice man."

Carrie smiled. "Glen is very nice. Carl and I were good friends with Glen and Wilma for a lot of years. It was devastating for all of us when she died."

"It sort of sounded like Glen and his wife didn't get along all that well," I pointed out.

"Far from it. Glen loved his wife, and she adored him. There was an odd ritual between them when it came to picking out furniture for the house. I didn't really understand it, but I could see that it came from a place of love. I suspect that at some point early on in their relationship, one of them purchased something the other one hated, which seemed to initiate a game of sorts that resulted in some rather odd choices over the years. But I never picked up on any real tension between them, and when Wilma got sick, Glen put his life on hold to be there for her." She took a sip of her wine. "I'm very happy with my decision to move, but I will miss having Glen right across the street. He's a good person and easy to talk to."

"You can always invite him over. Maybe you could start having weekly dinners together or something like that," I suggested.

Her expression grew contemplative. "Yes, maybe. We do share a long history. He knows all my secrets, and I know his. We've been there for each other through the best and the worst of times. I'd really hate to lose what we have." She shook her head and then smiled, almost as if she'd pulled herself from a trance. "So, where is Quinn, and what have the two of you been up to today?"

"Quinn is with Sam. I doubt we'll see her until tomorrow. As for what we've been up to today, I have what I suspect will be somewhat of a shocking story to tell you."

She raised a brow. "Shocking how?"

"I left you a note this morning letting you know that Quinn and I had gotten up early and were going to see Sam. We both felt the need to come clean about our adventure last night."

"Yes, I got the note and was happy you were going to fill him in. How'd he take it?"

"He was upset at first, but things ended up working out. The three of us actually managed to garner an invite to the island."

"Did you find Grace?" Carrie asked.

"No, but we did find Peggy."

After explaining that Peggy didn't want anyone other than us to know where she was, I spent the next thirty minutes catching her up on everything Peggy had shared with us. It was a difficult and emotional thirty minutes since Carrie was as shocked as Quinn and I had been about what had been going on with Peggy before her disappearance, and her choice to run away from her problems rather than staying to face them. I supposed that after thinking about it, I didn't really blame her. At first, I'd felt bad that she hadn't trusted us enough to share what was going on, but when I thought about the fact that she had shared her situation with both her mother and her brother and they'd shut her down, I realized she actually had a really good reason not to trust or expect help from anyone.

"I had no idea any of that was going on," Carrie said, wiping a tear from her eye. "Maybe we should have. She'd been acting so oddly that summer. We attributed her behavior to her friendship with Dusty, but maybe as her best friends, we should have known."

"I remember that she pulled away from us that summer," I said. "I get it now, but at the time, I remember feeling slighted by her. She seemed to have this whole other life she didn't want to share with us. At the time, I thought that other life revolved around her age-inappropriate boyfriend, and I was irritated. But now that I know what was really going on, I realize I wasn't there for her the way I should have been."

"We couldn't have known," Carrie said. "The idea that her father was doing what he was is just so strange. The guy was an attorney. He was involved in politics. He seemed so normal." She paused. "Although I do remember being intimidated by him. He had a very assertive presence. And I do remember

Peggy being afraid of him and much happier when he wasn't around, but I thought that was just because he was strict, whereas her mother was always sick and never seemed to get out of bed, let alone pay much attention to what Peggy was doing."

"I suppose that her real illness might have been depression brought on by guilt," I said. "She died a couple of years after Peggy went missing. I heard she'd had an accident, but there had been rumors that her death had actually been the result of suicide. At the time, I remember thinking that if it had been suicide, it had been over the loss of her child, and maybe it was, but maybe it had more to do with guilt over her failure to help that child when she had the chance. She must have been in so much pain."

"If she felt pain for not helping Peggy, then I actually find I'm glad about that," Carrie said. "That may seem mean, but in this situation, all my sympathy goes to Peggy. She must have been so terrified and lost and lonely."

"I'm sure she was."

"Does she seem happy now?" Carrie asked.

I nodded. "She did seem happy. She said several times that she felt safe with Wilson. I suppose that after living in a situation where you are powerless and never felt safe, feeling safe is a biggie in terms of what you feel you need to survive. She indicated that she had no desire to leave the island, although she was welcome to do so at any time. I guess I get that. Her father is a monster. When she was younger, she was afraid he would find her, and she'd be forced to go back. At some point, she must have convinced herself that she was only safe as long as she was on the island, so she simply stayed."

Carrie closed her eyes and tilted her face in the direction of the sun. "Having a sense of security is important. Maybe even the most important thing. When you have it, you don't even realize how much you need it, but when it's gone, it can leave you feeling like you are adrift in an angry sea. I get not wanting to rock the boat once you find a safe haven. I'm sure it was easier to stay."

"I'm sure it was," I agreed.

Carrie opened her eyes and looked at me. "You know the memory of that summer we all went camping up at Jordan's Peak comes to mind. It seems to me it was early in the summer at least a month before Peggy went missing."

"I remember," I said.

"The part of that memory that sticks out for me is the night we played truth or dare. I remember that Peggy picked dare every time even though Quinn kept giving her ridiculous dares. Quinn seemed determined to ask Peggy about Dusty, so she wanted her to choose truth, but Peggy stuck to her guns, only choosing dare while Quinn made her eat a worm and strip naked and yodel at the moon."

"I remember that I kept telling Peggy to pick truth. I felt bad for her. Quinn can be mean at times. Or at least she could be mean back then. I suppose I also wanted to ask Peggy what was up with Dusty, who, if you remember, we all thought she was sleeping with."

"As it turns out, I guess it wasn't Dusty who was sleeping with her," Carrie said.

I placed my hand on my stomach. "This whole thing makes me sick. I'm glad I know that Peggy is okay, but I sort of wish I didn't know the rest. I know it's crazy to do so, but I feel really guilty that we didn't realize what was going on and help her."

"I know," Carrie said. "I feel the same way. I wish I could say there weren't signs, but there were. We knew something was going on. She was withdrawn and pushing us away. We suspected that Peggy had been sexually intimate and was feeling guilty and ashamed about that. We just missed the mark on knowing who had been causing so much trauma in her life."

Carrie was right. There had been signs. A lot of them. We were just too young and innocent to be able to read them.

"So what are you up to tonight? Do you have plans with Ryder?" Carrie asked, changing the subject to something less depressing, which I was grateful for.

"Actually, I do. Although I feel bad about leaving you here all alone. I could cancel, but I do need to tell him about our trip and finding Peggy before he hears it from someone else. Maybe I should just invite him over here."

"Nonsense. I'm a big girl who can look out for herself. I have a bottle of wine in the refrigerator and a movie I taped last week that I've been wanting to watch. You go and have fun."

"Are you sure?" I asked.

"Of course, I'm sure. At first, after Carl left, it was hard to be alone in the house so often, but I am alone, so I guess I need to get used to it. Before you arrived, I was going out almost every night as a way of avoiding the silence, but I can see now that my inability to spend time alone was going to turn into a real problem. Maybe I'll call Jessica and see how her trip is going."

"It's late there. In fact, it's the middle of the night there."

Carrie rolled her lips. "I guess you make a good point. But seriously, don't worry about me. I can entertain myself just fine."

"Okay," I said, still feeling uncertain. "I shouldn't be too late. I'm actually pretty tired after last night, so my plan is to come clean with Ryder, enjoy a meal, and then have an early night." I stood up and then paused. "I forgot to mention that Peggy knew Hillary Denton. I know she was a full-time resident, and you've always lived here, so I figured you might remember her disappearance."

"I remember. Her parents were devastated when she disappeared."

"Peggy said that like her, Hillary came to the island to escape a bad situation. She said that Hillary was pregnant and wanted to keep her baby, but her parents forbid her from doing so. They told her that if she wouldn't agree to have an abortion, they'd take her baby from her as soon as it was born. Does that sound right? Were her parents that hard and unreasonable?"

Carrie paused. "My first instinct was to answer no, but thinking back, they were strict. I remember that Hillary had to go to the library where her mother worked after school, rather than taking the bus home. Her parents were the sort to want to put up a good front. They always acted as if things were perfect at home, but after Hillary disappeared, I do remember thinking that she'd probably just run away to escape her strict upbringing. I had no idea she was pregnant.

In fact, there were rumors about drug use, but if she loved her baby enough to fight for it, then I have to assume those rumors were false."

"Yeah," I agreed. "Drug use doesn't really fit in with wanting to keep your baby."

"Did Peggy know how things turned out for her?" Carrie asked.

"She had her baby, and after she turned eighteen, Wilson gave her some money and helped her get a new start."

"So the guy we both thought was creepy, is actually a nice guy."

"It sounds as if he is," I said. "I'm not saying that some of his choices aren't odd, but he does seem to have a big heart and a willingness to act on his compassion."

"I wonder why he keeps mistresses on Shipwreck Island. The guy is loaded. It seems like he could have a real relationship."

"I suppose we'd need to know the man a lot better than we do to answer that question." I slid my chair in and stepped away from the table. "Call me if you need anything. If not, I'll be home in a few hours."

Chapter 8

I'd originally planned to meet Ryder at the boathouse, but he called and offered to pick me up. When he arrived, he had his motorcycle instead of his truck, so I changed from my dress into a pair of shorts. I enjoyed riding on the back of his bike, but I'd noticed an unusual tension that had me feeling nervous tonight.

The ride along the coast was pleasant and relaxing. He took the scenic route, which dipped to the south then looped back around in a northerly direction. Eventually, we ended up at a seafood restaurant overlooking the sea. The view was gorgeous, the menu varied, and the atmosphere designed for romance, but my intuition told me that something was up.

"This is lovely, but I thought we'd talked about grabbing takeout and heading to the boathouse," I said once we'd been seated, and the wine had been ordered and poured.

"That is what we talked about," Ryder admitted, "but then I realized if we went to the boathouse, we'd probably end up doing something other than talking."

Okay, that had me frowning. "And you don't want to do something other than talking?" I asked, knowing that *other than talking* was code for sex, which I was very much interested in if we were able to get past the awkward conversation we needed to have regarding my trip with Quinn and Carrie to the island and the follow-up trip with Quinn and Sam.

"It's not that. Really. I am very much interested in doing something other than talking, it's just that something came up today that made me realize that I had something I wanted to talk to you about. I also realized this particular conversation would be better accomplished at a restaurant rather than the boathouse."

I suddenly realized what must be going on. "You spoke to Sam," I said. "You found out about our trip to the island, and you're mad, which is why you didn't want to have an intimate dinner at the boathouse."

"I did talk to Sam," Ryder confirmed, "but I'm not mad. I was a little hurt at first, but after I thought about things, I realized that I understood why you did things the way you did. If I'm honest, I wish that you would have trusted me enough to confide in me, but I am happy you found Peggy and thrilled that she's okay. Having said all of that, the thing I want to talk to you about has nothing to do with Peggy or your trip last night."

I took a sip of my wine. "Okay. Then what does it have to do with?"

Ryder looked nervous, which was odd. He was an easygoing sort of guy, who seemed to take things as they came. Being nervous wasn't a behavior I associated with him, but he was frowning, and there was definitely a look of concern on his face.

"I spoke to the town clerk today, and we discussed the fact that the town's computer system is in serious need of an upgrade. Not only is our webpage seriously out of date, but the interface that allows those who visit to link to hotels, transportation, dining, and other services is pretty antiquated as well. We've basically decided to commit the funds and upgrade to something we can be proud of, and it occurred to me that you might be the perfect person to head up the project."

Now, it was my turn to frown. "You brought me here to this restaurant rather than to the boathouse because you want to offer me a job?"

"No." He hesitated. "I mean, sure if you're interested in the job, you really would be perfect, but it's not just that. The job won't even start until after Labor Day."

I waited while he stumbled through, saying whatever it was that was actually on his mind.

"It was the fact that you are exactly the sort of person we would be looking for that got me to thinking about the fact that by Labor Day, you'll be gone. I guess that's what I really want to talk about."

I waited, not really knowing what to say.

He took my hand in his. "I know we've never discussed our relationship in any depth. We've never discussed what it might mean or where it might be headed. But when faced with the reality of a future without you, I realized I wanted you to be part of all my tomorrows and not just the next couple of weeks. I know when we started down this path, we both did so with the understanding that you'd just be here for part of the summer. I know that your life is in flux, and you have a lot to think about, but I'm hoping you will at least consider the idea of staying." He paused, looking at me with hope in his eyes. "I'm not trying to complicate things for you, and I don't expect an answer tonight, but I wanted you to know how I feel before you decide what your next move might be." He frowned. "I'm assuming that you haven't already made a decision about what you might do once your five weeks here come to an end."

"No," I said. "I haven't decided. I still have my apartment in the Bay, but I really don't see myself ever being happy there now that Kayla is gone. My old boss wants me to come back, but I'm pretty sure I'm done with that as well. Carrie did suggest that I might want to stay here on the island, but we never discussed it in depth. I'm sure I can crash in her new guest room if I need time to think things over once the five-week lease on the rental is up."

"So, you've considered it?"

I nodded. "I have. But I suspect there's more going on here than the fact that you'll miss me if I decide to go back to the Bay."

He rubbed his thumb over my hand. "There is more going on. I'm pretty sure I'm falling in love with you. I guess I've known that for a little while, but I didn't want to say as much because I didn't want to put pressure on you to consider me or my feelings as you make your decisions. I really want you to do what is best for you. And I know this conversation might seem to have come out of left field, it's just that, today, when the job situation came up, and I thought about you leaving, I realized how very much I wanted you to stay. I thought about it all day, and in the end, I decided that I needed to say something. I needed you to know that if staying is something you might be interested in, then I might be interested in taking our relationship to the next level."

"And what level might that be?" I asked, tilting my head slightly.

He smiled. "I don't know. Maybe we could go steady."

I laughed. "It's been a while since a boy asked me to go steady. Can I get back to you?"

"Absolutely."

I leaned across the table and kissed him. "Now that we have that discussion out of the way, what do you say we get our order to go and head to the boathouse after all?"

He ran a finger along my jaw, pausing at my lips. "We haven't ordered yet, so maybe we'll just skip the food. I'll get the check and pay for the wine."

Chapter 9

I woke with a smile on my face. Although I'd never actually said as much, nor was I ready to do so, after thinking about my conversation with Ryder, I realized that he wasn't the only party in the relationship falling in love. To this point, my life had been all about my sister and my career. I'd certainly dated and had even had a few meaningful relationships along the way, but I'd never been interested in finding someone to build a life with. My long-term plan had always been to grow old with Kayla, but now that she was gone, I realized that staying here on the island with Ryder and Carrie, where I'd been happier than I'd been for a very long time, was an idea that appealed to me quite a lot.

Rolling over, I looked out the window as the first rays of the sun turned the sky to wispy shades of pink and purple. The fog had rolled in by the time Ryder had finally brought me home, but apparently, it had rolled out again at some point during the overnight hours. I sat up and grabbed a warm sweatshirt to pull over the shorts and tank top I'd worn to bed. Opening my window, I looked out at the calm sea as the waves lapped onto the beach. Ryder and I had agreed not to meet up for our morning run since he had an early surgery, and I wasn't getting home until well into the wee hours of the early morning, but I found the lure of the quiet morning more than I could resist. Stepping away from the window, I pulled on running shorts, a sports bra, and a clean tank top, and after grabbing my shoes and socks, I headed outside into the crisp morning air.

Settling into a comfortable pace, I let my mind wander. The conversation with Ryder had started out awkward and had continued down a somewhat rocky path as he'd tried to find the words to convey what he needed to say, but once he got the words out there on the table, and his meaning had become clear, our evening had taken on a different feel entirely. Making love with Ryder last night, knowing that he felt the same strong emotions for me that I felt for him, was something I'd never really experienced before. When Kayla had tried to explain the difference between an act of intimacy between two people with a true emotional connection and an act of intimacy between two people simply looking for companionship or tension release, I'd honestly thought she'd been making things up, but as it turned out, I was wrong.

The sun peeked over the distant mountain as I merged onto the hard sand where Ryder and I normally ran. I missed him being here this morning, but I did understand his commitment to his patients, and I understood that being a man with many talents and interests, his time was in high demand. I thought about how it would be to live here on the island and to see him every day. I also thought about how it would feel to leave, should that be my ultimate decision. Last night, the decision seemed complicated, but somehow this morning in the bright light of day, it seemed obvious. Turning around, I headed back toward the house. It seemed that perhaps I needed to have a chat with Carrie.

When I returned to the house, I found Carrie sitting on the back deck with a cup of coffee. Our morning chats were a ritual I'd come to enjoy.

"Good morning," she said. "How was your run?"

"It was nice. Quiet since Ryder had a surgery and wasn't able to join me." I sat down across from her. "Did Quinn ever make it home?"

"Not as far as I know. There are muffins on the counter to go with the coffee."

"Thanks, but coffee is fine for now."

"So how was your dinner?" she asked.

I thought of the peanut butter and jelly sandwiches we'd eventually settled on. "Actually, it was perfect. I'm sorry I didn't make it home as early as I'd planned."

"No need to apologize." She smiled. "Like I said, I'm a big girl. I can spend a few hours in the house alone."

I tucked my legs up under my body. "I know. It's just that you planned this awesome get together for the four of us, and it seems that ever since we've been here, we've all been bailing on you."

Carrie lifted a corner of her mouth. "It's not a problem. I'm glad you and Quinn are having fun. I'm hoping Nora is working things out with Matt, and I am thrilled we found Peggy alive and well. All in all, it's been a better reunion than I'd imagined it might be. Besides, I've spent more than my share of time at the new condo, so perhaps it's me who is ignoring you."

I smiled. "I'm really happy you found the condo. You seem a lot happier since making the decision to move."

"I am a lot happier, although I am really going to miss you and Quinn when you go."

"Yeah, about that," I said, setting my coffee mug on the table in front of me. "I'm thinking I might stay for a while beyond the five weeks. If I do, how would you feel about letting me rent your guest room?"

Carrie grinned. "Are you thinking about staying permanently?"

"Perhaps."

"I'd love for you to stay, and the guest room is yours for as long as you want, no need to pay rent. I certainly don't need the income."

"Thank you. I have a lot of decisions to make, and I really haven't figured it all out, but what I have figured out is that, other than my nieces, who are both off at college, everyone I care about is here."

"What about your mother?" Carrie asked.

"Yes, I guess I do care about her, but we do better if we maintain a certain distance, and San Francisco is close enough that I can visit whenever I want."

"Well, I, for one, would be thrilled to have you stay." She paused. "Have you discussed this with Ryder?"

"He's actually the one who brought it up. He even asked me to go steady."

She laughed. "Steady? Really?"

"It was a joke, but I knew what he was really trying to say without putting me on the spot. He wants us to have a real relationship and not just a summer fling. I wasn't sure how I felt about his suggestion at first, but the more I think about it, the more I realize that staying is what I want as well. He did hint at one point that I could just move in with him, but I think it might be better to stay in your guest room until I have a chance to think things through. The last thing I want to do is get into something I'm not ready for. Actually, that's the second to the last thing I want. The last thing I want is to hurt him."

"And you know I don't want either of you hurt," Carrie said.

"I know." I tucked my hair behind my ear. "But I don't think that's where we're headed. I really think Shipwreck Island is where I'm meant to be. I'm not exactly sure what I want to do about a career, but whatever I end up doing, I can clearly imagine Ryder by my side."

Carrie reached over and gave me a hug.

"So, what's on the agenda for today?" I asked once we had that settled.

"I don't have specific plans," Carrie answered. "I spoke with Nora last night. She said things with her and Matt are going great. He's going to drop her off here on Saturday. She plans to attend the regatta with us on Sunday and maybe spend a few days beyond that on the island, but then she plans to go home and continue to work on her marriage."

"That's great. I'm happy to hear it."

"We have this house leased for another two weeks. Quinn has never said how long she plans to stay. I'm hoping she'll stay the entire time. If you're serious about staying on the island, I guess you'll need to do something about your apartment, but there's time to consider that. I guess the most important thing for me at this point is to make sure that all my friends are settled and happy."

"You don't always have to be the one to take care of everyone else," I pointed out.

"Actually, I think I do. It's my role in the group dynamic." Carrie looked at her watch. "I'm surprised Quinn isn't back. Sam must be headed to work by now."

She had a point. "I'll text her and get an update. I know Sam indicated that he was really tired when we split up yesterday, but I also know that he's pretty determined to find Grace before the weekend. At least that's what he said during one of his more passionate moments."

"Do you think she's okay?" Carrie asked. "Do you think Grace is even alive?"

I nodded. "I do think she's okay. She may even have left home of her own free will. She was angry at her mother, and teen feelings can mutate and multiply if not kept in check."

"I guess, but she's been gone for five days. It seems like a long time to hold a grudge just because her mother wouldn't let her quit school and go pro."

"I suppose that's true, but I also suspect there is more going on. Lizzy hurt Grace," I replied. "In my opinion, the fact that she's been gone for five days probably has more to do with Lizzy obviously supporting Hope's goals and happiness over Grace's. I can't imagine what it must have been like to win such a huge competition, only to realize that instead of being proud of you, your mother was disappointed that your sister hadn't won."

"I guess I see your point," Carrie said. "Lizzy was pretty open about the fact that she was pulling for Hope. I suspect that same attitude might carry over into other areas of Grace's life. I do feel bad for her."

"Me too." Leaning back in my chair, I picked up my mug and took a sip of my coffee. "I wonder where she might go. If she really is just blowing off steam, chances are she's confided in someone." I stared out at the sea as I considered the situation. "I remember that Grace's best friend is named Loretta and that Sam has already spoken to her. Do you happen to know who Grace's other friends are?"

"I don't know," Carrie said. "But I bet Sam has already asked Lizzy that very question. I suppose we can call him and ask. We can check on Quinn at the same time."

Deciding that Carrie had a good idea, I called Sam, who shared that Lizzy had listed two teenage girls as being close to Grace in addition to Loretta. He confirmed that he'd already spoken to both girls. As for Quinn, he shared that she'd left in the middle of the night. He didn't know exactly where she'd gone, but he did know that she'd called a cab that she'd asked to bring her here to the house. I headed out to the front drive, only to verify that the car she'd borrowed from Carrie was gone.

"Where could she have gone?" Carrie asked.

"I have no idea. Sam had no idea. I sent a text. I guess we'll just have to wait and see if she texts back."

"It's weird that she left without saying anything," Carrie said. "I have to admit that I'm really worried.

Did Sam make it sound like they'd had a fight or something?"

"No," I answered. "He told me that they'd had a nice evening together and then they'd fallen asleep early. When he awoke, she was gone. Since he'd picked her up, he checked with the local cab company, and they told him that someone from his address had called for a ride around four a.m. The cab driver told him he'd dropped her off here at the house, so Sam assumed she just wanted to head home for some reason. He wasn't worried until I told him that both Quinn and Jessica's car were gone."

"I'm sure Quinn is fine," Carrie said. "Her boss has been hounding her to cover that summit going on over in San Francisco. Maybe she finally decided to give in and do what he asked."

"Maybe," I said. "I'm sure she'll call when she can. In the meantime, let's make some breakfast. I'm starving."

Carrie had come across a recipe for a breakfast casserole in one of the magazines she subscribed to, so while she made that, I cut up some fruit for a salad.

"I think we need to celebrate the fact that you've decided to stay here on the island with mimosas," Carrie said, pulling out a bottle of champagne.

"Sounds good to me."

"Does Ryder know you're staying?" she asked as she poured orange juice over the bubbly.

"Not yet. He made his case and then asked that I think about it before answering. I agreed to do that, so we changed the subject. I really thought it would take me days to decide, but I woke up this morning and just knew. He's getting off at three today since he went in early, so I guess I'll head over to his place when he gets off and talk to him about it." I took a sip of the fruity drink. "Believe it or not, he started off a discussion about his feelings for me and his desire that I stay here on the island with a job offer."

"A job offer?" Carrie laughed. "You're kidding, right?"

"No. I'm afraid not. I could see he was nervous, and I guess I don't blame him. He couldn't have known how I'd react to what he had to say. I suppose, in his mind, giving me a reason to stay by offering a job made sense."

"So are you going to take it? The job, I mean?"

"No," I answered. "The work sounds routine and boring, and to be honest, I don't really need the income. At least, not right now. I think I'll take my time and get settled before I decide where to commit my time. If I am going to work, I want to find something meaningful. In the meantime, I'll just hang out with you, do some surfing, and maybe get back in touch with the part of myself that always wanted to be a writer."

She slipped the casserole in the oven. "I can't even begin to tell you how happy I am about this. I've missed you. I've missed all of you, but especially you."

"I know. I've missed you too."

Chapter 10

Quinn finally called an hour later. We'd eaten our breakfast and were cleaning the kitchen by this point, although there were plenty of leftovers if Quinn was hungry, so I told her as much.

"I'm not on the island," she said. "But, the casserole sounds yummy, so please save me some."

"Did you decide to cover the event in San Francisco like your boss wanted?" I asked.

"Actually, no," Quinn answered. "I have an idea where Grace might be. I can't be sure until I check it out, but let's just say I have a hunch."

"Where do you think she is?" I asked.

"LA. Well, Malibu, actually."

"LA?" I glanced at Carrie, who was hanging on my every word. "Why would you think Grace is in LA?"

"Carl told Sam that Grace called him on Saturday night, asking about a house he had for sale that Rain owns. She obviously hadn't seen the house yet, nor had her friend, since she told Carl they wanted the address so they could drive by. This indicates to me that the reason they were interested in the house was because of who owned it and not because of the merits of the house itself."

I took a minute to process this. "Okay, I get it. If they hadn't seen the house, the friend couldn't know he or she was interested unless the reason they were interested was because of who owned it. But a lot of people I can think of would be interested in viewing the home of a celebrity. How does this help you know who Grace was with?"

"I don't know for sure," Quinn said. It sounded like she was on her Bluetooth. If I had to guess, she was cruising south as we spoke. "But I did remember that Sam mentioned that the house had been broken into. If the person with Grace was a legitimate buyer interested in viewing the home, he or she would have called the Realtor whose name was given to Grace by Carl. Since they didn't call this woman and broke a window to get in, it makes sense that they had a reason to want to get into the house that had nothing to do with a home purchase. I asked myself what that reason might be, and settled on the most obvious reason — theft."

"I get what you are saying, but I still don't see how this helps us find Grace."

"I'm getting to that," Quinn said. "When we were at the surfing competition, I noticed Grace talking to Skeet Fairbanks. Skeet, as you know, is a professional surfer with a bunch of high dollar endorsements that have brought him a lot of money. What you may not know is that Skeet used to date a model named Rebeka. Based on what I know, they were actually quite serious until Rebeka met Rain at a party and fell madly in love with the charismatic musician."

"So Skeet had reason to want to do harm to Rain," I said. "I guess I can see where you're going with this to a point. Skeet and Grace chat during the four days of competition and perhaps become friends of sorts. Skeet knows that Rain has a house on the island he's trying to sell, but he doesn't know where on the island the house might be located. Given the nature of the sale, and the fact that it is owned by a celebrity, the address most likely isn't listed on the listing agreement provided on the internet or in ads, so Grace volunteers to call Carl and get the address. Once they have the address, they break in and steal something, which I have to assume Skeet knows is valuable to Rain, and then what? It seems like Grace's role would be fulfilled at this point. Why do you think she's in LA?"

"Skeet has a place in Malibu. I really don't know for certain that Grace is there, but it seemed reasonable to me that if Grace helped Skeet and she needed a place to hang out while she worked out her anger and disappointment over her mother's obvious preference for her older sister, he might invite her to hang out with him for a while. I've been to the mansion. It has a lot of rooms, and there are always a lot of people hanging around, partying, and whatnot."

"But Grace is sixteen," I pointed out. "He'd be crazy to help her run away."

Quinn blew out a breath. "Yeah, there is that, and Skeet doesn't appear to me to be a stupid man, but it was an idea to check out, and I had some time, so I decided to follow my intuition. I'll be back on the island tomorrow either way."

"Call me when you get to Malibu. I'm curious as to what you find."

"I will," Quinn promised. "If Grace is with Skeet, I'll bring her back with me. If not, then I wasted a couple of days chasing a dead end. It wouldn't be the first time."

Once I hung up, I filled Carrie in.

"Do you really think a rich and connected guy like Skeet would use a sixteen-year-old to help him break into someone's house?" she asked.

"I don't know," I admitted. "Love can make you do crazy things, and Quinn made it sound as if Skeet and Rebeka were serious before Rain came into the picture. If he wanted to steal something but didn't want anyone to know that he stole it, he wouldn't have made the call to get the address himself. It would be too obvious. While Skeet might be an adult, that doesn't mean he's mature. The guy is what, twenty-five? I've seen him on TV. He looks and sounds like a teenager most of the time with his surfer-dude vibe. If Grace struck up a conversation with him and he needed her help, I could see him making a deal of some sort with her."

"If Quinn is right and Skeet did break into Rain's house to steal something, what could he have possibly wanted?"

I shrugged. "I have no idea."

"And how did he get past the security system? I'm assuming the house must have one."

"Again, I really don't know, but I seem to remember Sam saying something about the security system being remotely disabled."

"Should we tell Sam what's going on?" Carrie asked.

"No. Not yet. I suppose it's up to Quinn to fill him in when she's ready. She said she'd call when she gets to Malibu, which I suppose should be in three or four hours based on the distance she has to travel. If she took the early ferry, she would have hit the terminal on the other side shortly before six. At this point, I guess we just wait."

Carrie frowned but agreed. She indicated that she was going to go upstairs to shower and dress and then planned to head over to the condo. She asked if I wanted to come along. I found that I wanted that very much. She offered to put the furniture she had slated for the guest room into storage if I wanted to bring my own furniture to the island, but it seemed like a lot of trouble to do that at this point, so I told her I'd just use what she had until I figured out what I was going to do on a long-term basis.

As I showered, I thought about Carrie's suggestion to call Sam. My initial reaction was to wait and let Quinn fill him in, but I knew he was worried, and now that I had opened the box and informed him that Quinn was not here at the house, I felt like I had to tell him something. After a bit of going back and forth with myself, I decided to call him and at least tell him where she was.

"I spoke to Quinn," I said after he answered. "She's actually on her way to LA. She told me to tell you that she will call you this evening and will be home tomorrow."

"I wonder why she didn't mention that she was going to be away when we saw each other last night."

I had to admit that Sam sounded hurt that Quinn had kept her trip to herself.

"I think it was a last-minute thing. She didn't mention anything to Carrie or me either. In fact, she didn't even leave a note. I suppose we should be irritated by that, but Quinn is a bit of a lone wolf. She always has been. I don't think it comes naturally to her to consider others when it comes to deciding where to go or what to do."

"Yeah, she's mentioned on several occasions that she pretty much just does whatever she feels she needs to do to get the story she's after and rarely checks in with anyone else," Sam said. "If she doesn't call me by the time I get back from my interviews, I'll try calling her."

"Interviews?" I asked.

"I've arranged to speak to the people that Lizzy named as being closest to Grace a second time. When I spoke to them the first time, they claimed to have no idea where she was, and maybe that was true. But after we spoke, I realized it was likely that Grace would have said something to someone if she had voluntarily left the island as we hope."

I leaned a hip against a table as I looked out the window. "Yeah, it does seem that she would have called or texted her closest friends at some point. I get why she might be hurt and angry and why she might want to retaliate against her mom by doing something to cause her pain and worry, but I don't think she'd want to worry her friends."

I thought about Peggy and the fact that she simply disappeared, hurting everyone, including her friends, but her case was different. She had a huge secret much too big to share, and she was terrified of being found by her family. If Grace had simply taken off out of anger, my bet was that she planned to return on her own, probably sooner than later.

"Any new leads on Veronica Smith's death?" I asked. "We now know where she'd been the past five years or at least the majority of the past five years, and we know she had opium plants, which could mean she planned to meet up with someone who deals in illegal drugs. To me, that seems like a motive, although I'm not sure how much good that will do us if we don't know who might have been in the market for the plants."

"I actually have a couple of ideas to check out," Sam said. "As I said before, most of the illegal opiates in the area are imported from countries to our south. Still, I know of a couple of people who might know if someone was looking to buy the plants."

"Okay, be careful."

"I will be. The reality is that we don't even know for certain Veronica was murdered. We know she drowned, but she could have ended up in the water for a number of reasons. I do intend to follow the clues as far as I can, but finding Grace is what I'm most concerned about."

"I know. Hopefully, we'll have her home by the weekend."

After I hung up with Sam, I went out onto the deck to wait for Carrie. It was such a gorgeous day that I hated to spend one more minute inside than I absolutely needed to. I really had no idea why I hadn't visited the island more often than I had over the years. I'd always loved it here, and I still had friends I would have enjoyed connecting with. The fact that I could count on one hand the number of times I'd traveled to the island during the twenty-four years between graduating high school and arriving for this visit was actually pretty sad.

"Are you ready?" Carrie asked, poking her head out the back door.

"I am. Should we take both cars? Are you planning on moving boxes?"

"Actually, I'm going to work on organizing what I've already moved, so we can ride over together. If you want to text Ryder and tell him to just meet us at the condo when he gets off, that would work for me."

"Okay. I will. I'm excited to set up my temporary room. I'll need to make a trip back to the Bay to pack up my apartment and give notice, but I suppose I can do that after Quinn and Nora leave."

I climbed into the passenger side of Carrie's car. "Do you think we should still go camping now that we know Peggy is alive, and a memorial for her seems sort of silly?"

"I don't know," Carrie answered. "We could focus the memorial on Kayla."

I frowned. "I don't know if I really want to do that. Not yet. It's still all too raw and fresh."

"I understand. We could go camping minus the memorial aspect, but I guess we should ask Quinn and Nora on Saturday when Nora gets here. Nora sounded like she planned to spend less than a week with us, so I guess we should find out what she'd like to do." Carrie paused. "I wonder if there's any way we can arrange a visit with Peggy. All of us."

"I don't know. I know access to the island is really limited, so hopping over for a visit probably isn't in the cards. But she did say she was free to come and go if she wanted to. I know that she feels safe in her current environment, and she made it clear she has no desire to leave, but maybe we could get her to agree to meet up with us for the day. If not alone, maybe we could speak to Wilson about bringing her here to meet us, or maybe we could meet up with him and Peggy on his yacht. It's a discussion worth having."

"I'd love to see her. I'm sure Nora would as well. Do you have a way to contact her?"

"No, but Sam has Wilson's contact information. Maybe we could ask him to contact Wilson on our behalf once Nora gets here, and this thing with Grace is wrapped up."

"Did you tell her about Kayla?" Carrie asked.

"No. Our time together was short, and the timing seemed off. She didn't ask about anyone. She simply told Quinn and me what she felt she needed to share, and then she ended the visit. Maybe if we can arrange a second visit, we can catch her up."

Chapter 11

Quinn called several hours later as Carrie and I were loading the empty boxes we'd unpacked into the back of her car for disposal at the recycling center. She'd informed me that she'd been able to talk to Skeet, who admitted that he had made a deal with Grace to give her a ride to LA in exchange for helping him to steal the sex tapes of Rain and Rebeka he knew were kept at Rain's home on Shipwreck Island. He wasn't certain they'd be in the location Rebeka had told him about during one of their drunken arguments since the house had been listed for sale, but he figured the risk was low since Rain wasn't on the island, so he might as well take a look.

"Sex tapes? Really?" Carrie said once I'd filled her in. "Talk about successful men who act like children. What was Skeet thinking? He could be charged with kidnapping. He must know that."

"I had the same thought, but to be honest, I'm not sure doing jail time for helping Grace ever occurred to him," I said. "Skeet seems to be a personality type I refer to as a Peter Pan. The carefree little boy who never grows up no matter what his age or level of financial success he might achieve. I knew a guy who was an actor when I lived in New York. He was fun and spontaneous and could party all night, but I swear I know fifteen-year-olds who make better choices than he did. For him, it was all about fun. Every decision was evaluated by the fun factor. And this guy was in his forties. I have no idea how he survived his own choices since most of the time, he was pure nuts, but somehow he got by, and to be honest, he seemed happy. I wouldn't choose to live my life the way he did, but despite the fact he was about as crazy as they come, he did seem to have fun."

"Yeah," Carrie sighed. "I guess I know a few guys like that." She closed her back door. "Okay, so we know Grace wanted to go to LA, and Skeet agreed to take her. Do we know why Grace wanted to go to LA?"

"She wanted to go and see her father."

"Grace is with Jake?" Carrie seemed surprised. "If Grace wanted to see her father, why didn't she just make arrangements for a visit? Why the disappearing act?"

"According to Quinn, Lizzy and Jake have been fighting, and Lizzy has refused to let Jake visit with Grace. The older girls can make their own decisions, of course, and it sounds as if neither is interested in visiting with Jake, but Grace told Skeet that her mother favors her sisters and that she's wanted to live with her dad for a while. When her mother found out that Grace had been talking to Jake about living with him, she cut off visitations all together."

"If that's true, it must have occurred to Lizzy that Grace might try to go to Jake," Carrie pointed out. "I wonder why she didn't tell Sam that right off the bat."

"I don't know," I admitted. "I guess you'll have to ask Lizzy that question if you're really interested. I've never been married, so I can't say for certain, but it does seem that relationship issues involving children can get tricky if both sides are determined to have their own way."

"Yes," Carrie said. "I suppose that's true. So is Quinn going to LA to find Jake and confirm that Grace is with him?" Carrie asked.

"No. She said she called Sam. The last thing she wanted to do was to get in the middle of a family drama. Sam spoke to Lizzy, who called and spoke to Jake, who confirmed that Grace was with him. According to Quinn, the official custody papers give Lizzy and Jake joint legal custody, so Sam and Quinn both agreed to let the ex-couple work it out."

"That makes sense to me." Carrie took her keys out of her purse. "Is Quinn on her way back?"

"Actually, she's meeting Sam in San Francisco. They're going to go to a couple clubs and spend some time together. Quinn said they'd be back before dinner on Saturday."

"I guess now that Grace has been found, the pressure is off, and Sam can take some time off."

"Sounds like it. He told me that he had a lead to follow up on relating to Veronica's death, but chances are once he does that, he'll call in his deputy to oversee things and head to the ferry."

"I'm glad Sam and Quinn made a connection," Carrie said, opening the driver's side door and sliding inside. "At first, I wasn't sure if the two of them getting together was a good idea given Quinn's temporary status on the island, but I'm sure Sam knows the score. Sam and Quinn both have stressful jobs, so it's good for them to have someone to blow off some steam with."

"But you were worried about Ryder and me," I pointed out, adjusting the air-conditioning vent on the passenger side.

"I was," Carrie admitted as she pulled away from the condo and headed toward the recycling center. "But Ryder is my baby brother, and he isn't Sam. Ryder has a tender heart. He feels deeply. This means that he can hurt deeply. I made it clear from the beginning that I didn't want to see him hurt."

"I know. I don't want him to be hurt either, and I guess if I'm honest, I had my doubts about a relationship between us when we were first getting started. I think one of the reasons I'm so attracted to him is because of the fact he's willing to lay it all on the line. He can overthink things, which can make him awkward at times, but I know he really means what he says. The guy doesn't have a dishonest bone in his body."

"He really is one of the good guys." Carrie pulled into the drive and got into the drop off line. "Maybe we should stop in town and have a drink when we finish here." Once we were assigned a lane, she pulled in, and we began unloading the boxes in a bin marked for used cardboard.

"I'm game. I just want to call Ryder and let him know what we're doing in the event he gets off while we're at the bar."

"Tell him to join us if he gets off early. I was going to call him later, anyway. I have a few questions about the new bank accounts he helped me set up after Carl and I divided our assets. One of the accounts is a CD, and I'm not sure if I'm supposed to do something with it or let it roll over."

We both returned to the car once we'd emptied the cardboard. "You do realize that you should learn to do all this yourself, don't you?" I asked. "It's great Ryder is helping out, but I know you want to be independent."

"I know," she admitted. "At first, it was easier to let him handle things, but eventually, I would like to be able to manage my own life. Should we head to the Boho Bar and Grill? They should have the sandpit open, and there's usually shade at this time of the day."

"That sounds fun," I said, remembering what a disaster the night had been the first time Carrie had taken me there. "I've been wanting to try one of their fun appetizers."

"They have excellent margaritas if you're looking for something refreshing, and their crab wontons are to die for. Oh, and we have to try the shrimp, avocado, and lettuce wraps with the sweet Tai sauce. They do something to the cream cheese layer that's really unique."

I called Ryder while Carrie drove. He confirmed that he had only one more patient to see, and then, providing there were no emergencies, he'd turn things over to the brothers who lived at the veterinary hospital and meet us for a drink.

"These margaritas are really good," I said twenty minutes later, after slipping off my sandals and digging my bare feet into the warm sand. "Not at all sweet and syrupy."

"They use fresh lime rather than a mix," she informed me. "I used to get these all the time before I decided to switch to shots, which is a habit I'm totally over by the way. I was such a mess when you first got here, but now, I feel happy and hopeful for the future."

I held up my glass. "Here's to new beginnings."

She clicked her glass to mine. "Maybe if you stay, Quinn will visit more often."

"Maybe," I said. "But she hasn't visited me all that often up to this point. On average, I'd say we've spent time together in person maybe once every three years."

"That may be," Carrie said, "but between you and me both being here on the island and Sam lurking in the background, we might convince her to come around more often. I'd love it if we were all together for Christmas. Well, maybe not all of us. I suppose Nora will want to be with her family. But maybe you and I and Sam and Ryder can do something together. If Quinn will join us, that will be all the better."

"It's kind of odd to look six months into the future and picture us all here on the island. Last Christmas, with Kayla in the hospital, was a total blur. I'm not sure it even registered that it was Christmas. But before that, I'd go to Kayla's every year. Now that she's gone, I'm glad I won't be alone this year."

"You don't think your nieces will come home for Christmas?" she asked.

I shrugged. "I don't know. Maybe, but even if they do, I think being with them would be weird for me. My brother-in-law is dating now. Even if the girls are there, which I honestly sort of doubt, it would be strange to see Mark with someone else." I took a sip of my drink. "When I think of spending Christmas with them without Kayla, I feel sad, but when I think of spending Christmas with you, Sam, and Ryder, I feel excited."

She took my hand in hers and gave it a squeeze. "I'm happy to hear that, but don't lose touch with your nieces. I think you'll regret it if you do."

"Once I get settled, I'd like to rent the house we're staying in now and have them both come to the island for a week or two. Maybe in the fall. I think a visit without overpowering memories or expectations of a holiday will be a better sort of visit for all of us."

"I think you're right, and a visit in the fall would be really nice. The summer crowds will have gone, yet the weather will still be nice. Maybe Jessica will even come home. I think she's about the same age as your older niece."

"She is. I think Jessica would get along splendidly with my nieces. I'm sort of surprised that you and Kayla hadn't gotten them together before this."

"Kayla visited the island even less often than you have over the years. In fact, I think the only times she even came were a couple of times she came with you. I remember you were both here for your thirtieth birthdays, but I'm not sure Kayla ever made it back after that."

"She was busy," I said. "She had a husband and two little girls. I guess hanging out with friends she knew from childhood hadn't been a big theme with her. Not like it is, and always has been with you, who kept tabs on everyone even after we all left."

"It was really depressing when you all stopped summering here. Sure, I had Carl, and overall I was happy, but I missed my friends. I missed being part of the Summer Six."

I smiled. "Yeah, me too. I'm glad I'm back. This really does feel right."

Carrie raised her arm and waved. "Ryder just showed up."

"I haven't told him I'm staying yet. I'd like to do so in private, so please don't bring it up unless he does."

"Of course. We'll all share a drink, and then I'll make myself scarce."

"You don't have to leave."

"No. It's okay. I have a few things to take care of anyway."

Chapter 12

"I feel bad that we chased Carrie off," I said to Ryder after she left, and the two of us decided to take a walk along the beach north of his boathouse.

"It sounded to me as if she had things to do," he said, entwining his fingers with mine as the warm water washed over our bare feet.

"I think that was an excuse to leave us alone. I wouldn't feel as bad if Quinn or Nora were here, but Nora is still in Mendocino with Matt, and Quinn is in San Francisco with Sam. Poor Carrie went to a lot of work to arrange this reunion, but it seems that we all keep bailing on her."

Ryder stopped walking. He turned so that we were facing each other. Leaning forward just a bit, he touched his lips to mine. "Do you want to head over to the rental so Carrie won't be alone?"

I paused as his breath caressed my face. "Actually, no. Not yet. I have something to talk to you about."

He took a step back and looked me in the eye. "Something bad?"

"No," I shook my head, "something good. But I wanted to talk to you alone so I could be certain we were on the same page."

"Okay." I could sense the hesitation in his voice. "What's going on?"

I took a breath, hoping that I was making the right choice and that I wouldn't end up looking back on this moment with regret. "I spoke to Carrie today about the idea of me staying on the island beyond the two weeks left on the lease for the rental."

He smiled.

"She agreed that I could move into the guest room in the condo on a temporary basis," I continued. "At this point, it feels like Shipwreck Island is the place I am meant to be, but I want to be sure you understand that my staying does not imply a commitment of any sort between the two of us. At least not yet."

His smile faded. "You want us to stop seeing each other?"

"No." I touched his face. "That isn't what I mean. I have feelings for you that I want to explore, and I enjoy spending time with you and knowing that you will be part of my day. But my life is in flux, and I still need to figure some things out. I don't want to hurt you, and I'm afraid if I stay for now, and then later decide to go, that is exactly what I'll do."

He took both my hands in his and looked deeply into my eyes. "But you might decide to stay? For good, that is."

"I might, but I'm not there yet. I don't want us to get ahead of ourselves. I want to continue doing what we're doing without the urgency to make life-altering decisions before either of us is ready."

He pulled my arms around his waist and then placed his hands on my face. "So, you're turning down my job offer?"

I nodded, smiling. "I am. But there are other offers you might be inclined to make that I might be inclined to take you up on."

He lifted me into his arms, calling to Baja, and then he carried me back to the boathouse.

A long time later, we settled onto his deck to watch the sun dip into the sea. I really couldn't remember the last time I'd felt this happy and this relaxed. Deep down inside, part of me knew that this is what I wanted for always and forever, but another part of me wanted to take it slow and make certain that I was able to make the commitment I knew Ryder wanted me to make.

"Sounds like your phone's ringing," Ryder said, getting up and walking into the house to fetch it.

"It's Quinn," I said after accepting the phone from his outstretched hand and checking the caller ID. "Hey, Quinn," I said after answering. "I wasn't expecting to hear from you. Is everything okay?"

"I'm not sure. I'm at the hotel where I was supposed to meet Sam more than two hours ago, but he never showed. I've tried calling him a half dozen times, but his phone goes straight to voicemail. I know he had a couple of people to talk to before he was going to head home to pack, but that was hours and hours ago. You haven't heard from him, have you?"

"No. Not since I spoke to him this morning."

"It's very odd that he isn't answering his phone. I mean, I get the fact that he might have gotten tied up and missed the ferry, but why wouldn't he call? I'm afraid something might have happened. Something bad. Can you and Ryder run over to his house and see if he's there? And, if he isn't there, can you check his office?"

"Yes. Absolutely. We'll go right now. I'll call you when we get there." I hung up and explained what was going on to Ryder. He tried to call Sam, but like it had for Quinn, his call went straight to voicemail. He left a message just in case, then he grabbed his wallet and keys, and we headed out the door.

"You don't think something happened to him, do you?" I asked as we sped down the coastal road toward his house.

Ryder's lips tightened. "I hope not, but it is odd that he's not answering his phone. Even if he ran out of battery and didn't have his charger, there's no way he'd simply stand Quinn up. He's crazy about her. Always has been. He would have found a way to call her no matter what the situation, unless, of course..."

"Unless, of course, he was physically unable to do so," I finished.

"Exactly." He pushed down even harder on the pedal. Ryder was the mayor, and he had a good reason for speeding, so I doubted he'd get a ticket, but going twice the speed limit was rarely a good idea. I pulled my seatbelt even tighter and hung on for dear life. "When you spoke to him earlier, did he say where he was going?" he asked as he slowed to merge onto the road that would take us into the neighborhood where Sam lived.

"He said he was going to speak to some of Grace's friends, but that was before Quinn found Grace. Quinn has talked to him since then, so whatever happened, assuming that something did happen, must have occurred after that point." I paused to remember. "He also mentioned having an idea who might have been interested in the opium plants Veronica stole from the commune up north. I'm not sure if he'd already followed up on that clue before Quinn spoke to him or not. I'll ask her when we call her back. Do you think we should call Sam's office?"

"It's closed by now. Central dispatch is in Sea Haven. They might know where Sam is or where he was heading, but let's check his home first. If he isn't there, we can drive over to his office."

Ryder pulled up in front of Sam's house and turned the ignition off.

"The house is dark, and his truck is gone."

"Yeah." Ryder opened his door. "Wait here. I know where he keeps his spare key. I'm going to take a look around."

"You don't want me to come with you?"

He shook his head. "It'd be best if I take a look alone. I'll only be a few minutes."

"Okay," I said, not understanding why Ryder didn't want me to come with him, but deciding that it wasn't a situation I cared about enough to get into an argument over.

Of course, waiting, even if for just a few minutes, was a lot harder than I thought it would be. Ryder had knocked on the door and rung the bell. When no one answered, he'd disappeared around the back. After a minute, I saw a light come on in the back of the house. I supposed the extra key might have been hidden somewhere in the backyard. Less than three minutes later, all the lights went off one by one in the opposite order from which they'd been turned on. Sixty seconds after the last one went off, Ryder joined me in the truck.

"He's not there," he said. "There's no sign of a struggle, so that's good. It doesn't look like he's been home since this morning, although he might have been in a hurry and didn't stop to clean up. Let's go by his office. If he isn't there, I'll call dispatch, and if they don't know where he is, we'll check a few of his favorite bars. Someone must have seen him at some point today."

"Maybe, but if he was working, he wouldn't have been in a bar," I pointed out.

"True. Maybe we can find his truck. I'm sure it has GPS. We should be able to track down the location of the truck, which hopefully is where Sam will be."

After we checked the office, which was closed up tight, Ryder called the central dispatch office on the east shore. The dispatcher on duty had come in after Sam had last called in, but he did share that according to the log, Sam had been headed to an address on the north shore to speak to a man named Cord Hannigan. Ryder asked if Sam had checked in at any point after that, and he shared that according to the log, he hadn't.

Ryder started the truck and headed back in the direction from which we'd come while I left yet another message for Sam and then called Quinn to fill her in. Of course, once I filled Quinn in on the fact that Sam wasn't at his house or office, she started to panic. She indicated that if we didn't find him in the next hour, she was going to charter a helicopter to bring her to the island since the last ferry had already left. Maybe she did care about Sam more than I'd suspected.

"So, do you know Cord Hannigan?" I asked Ryder as he sped north. "It seems like you know most of the people who live on this side of the island."

"I know Cord," he confirmed. "He owns a fishing boat out of the Hidden Harbor Marina. He's a crusty old guy who has zero tolerance for the growth and prosperity that has begun to change the local culture, and the two of us have had words on numerous occasions, but deep down, he's an okay sort of guy who is deeply entrenched in the idea of keeping everything exactly the same as it has always been."

"Why do you think Sam went to talk to him?" I asked.

Ryder narrowed his gaze. "I'm not sure. Cord is on the water pretty much every day, and he does know a lot of people. Maybe Sam had reason to believe he'd seen something."

When we arrived at Cord's house, I expected Ryder to tell me to wait in the truck once again, but this time, he invited me to talk to Cord with him. He pointed out that Cord was not a fan of him, but he certainly did have an eye for pretty women. I guess he hoped my being there would soften Cord up and get him to talk.

"Yeah, Sam was here," Cord confirmed after Ryder had introduced me and explained why we were there. "What of it?"

"He's missing, and we're trying to find out where he might be. What time was he here?" Ryder asked.

"I guess about two. He didn't stay long. Mentioned that he still had another stop to make, and he wanted to get off early today since he'd lined up a date for the evening."

"Do you know where he was going next?" I asked.

"Didn't say," Cord answered.

"Why was he here?" Ryder asked.

"Wanted to know about a fishing boat I might have seen last week. Not sure why he was trying to track it down, but when I mentioned that I'd seen a boat that looked a lot like the one he was looking for anchored near Horseshoe Island, he stepped outside to make a call."

"Do you know who he called?" Ryder asked.

"No idea. He didn't say, and I'm not a snoop."

"Is the boat still there?" Ryder asked.

Cord shrugged. "Don't know. Haven't been back up that way since I saw it."

"Did Sam say anything else that might indicate where he was going after he left here?" Ryder asked.

Cord immediately indicated that he hadn't.

"Please," I said. "Think about it for a minute. It's important."

Cord's eyes softened a bit when he looked in my direction. "He did say one thing that was odd. He asked me if I'd seen anyone hanging around the old hippie camp on Horseshoe Island. It's long gone now and wasn't there for more than a couple of years in the sixties since the island doesn't have a fresh water source, and hauling it in is a hassle. But there were a couple of summers where there was a group calling themselves Children of the Moon who built some structures, hauled in water, and called the place home.

They were known in the area for these weekend retreats where folks could pay a bunch of money to head out to the island, get stoned, have orgies, and find themselves."

I looked at Ryder. "Do you think Sam would have gone out to the island for some reason?"

"I'm not sure. He would have needed a boat. I happen to know the police boat is dry-docked for the weekend since Sam told me as much. I guess it needed servicing, and Sam didn't figure he'd need it over the weekend, so this was a good time to get it done. He wasn't expecting it to be ready to pick up until Monday, so he'd need to borrow a boat if he wanted to head out to the island. I would think he would call and ask to use mine, but he may have wanted a speed boat, so maybe he called Nick."

"Nick?" I asked.

He took my hand. "Come on. I'll fill you in on the way."

Ryder explained that Nick was a good friend of Sam's who happened to own one of the fastest boats on the island. Once we arrived at Nick's home and Ryder filled him in, he denied that Sam had called him about the boat, but offered to give the two of us a ride out to Horseshoe Island. Taking Nick up on his offer was the most expedient way to check out the situation, so Ryder agreed.

I called Quinn and filled her in. She really did seem frantic, but I was able to convince her that trying to charter a helicopter at this late hour was probably going to be a waste of time. After a bit of back and forth, I was finally able to convince her to wait at the hotel and take the early ferry in the morning. I also promised to call her with an update once we had a chance to check out the island.

The sea was calm this evening as was the wind, so the ride over to Horseshoe Island was pleasant enough. In fact, if I hadn't been worried about Sam, I would have enjoyed the feel of the boat gliding over the water as the warm air brushed my cheeks. Maybe if I decided to stay on the island permanently, I'd fork over some of my hard-earned savings to buy a boat. Of course, I was pretty sure Ryder would take me out on his boat any time I wanted, but skimming across the sea propelled by a powerful engine really was a different experience than gliding across the water propelled by the wind.

Nick slowed the boat as the island came into view. The first thing I did was look for a boat anchored in the area. Once it became apparent that there weren't any boats other than the one we were on, my attention focused on the barren landmass, which at this point, housed only ruins of the buildings that had once been erected by the hippies in the sixties.

"So, what now?" I asked Ryder. "It doesn't look like Sam is here."

Ryder frowned as he looked at the small island that was really shaped more like a half-moon than a horseshoe. "I'm not sure," he answered.

"If you want to take a look on the island, I can get you pretty close," Nick offered.

"I guess it couldn't hurt," Ryder said.

"You'll need to take your shoes off, but this boat is flat enough that I can bring it up to within a few feet of the shore."

By a few feet, Nick really meant about ten feet, but the water only reached Ryder's knees when he jumped out. Ryder had on shorts, but I had on long pants and didn't want them to get wet, so Ryder carried me from the boat to the shore. Nick waited with the boat. The island was small, and there wasn't really anything to search other than a few of the ruins, so we figured it wouldn't take long. It was dark, but Ryder and I each had a flashlight, so making our way across the sand was easy enough.

"It's pretty obvious no one is here," I said.

"Yeah, I know. I guess I just figured that as long as we'd come all the way out here, we might as well take a quick look around. While no one lives on the island, day-trippers do like to party in the area. Maybe we can find something that might give us a clue as to who might have been here today."

"Someone like Ernie Southern?" I asked, holding up a wallet.

Ryder took the wallet from my outstretched hand. He opened it and looked inside.

"I guess he might have been here partying," I said. "If his wallet fell out of his pocket, he might not have even realized it. Of course, he could have lost the wallet days ago, and hasn't thought to look for it here."

Ryder held up a ticket stub from the local cinema. "The ticket stub is from the night before last, which means that Ernie was here yesterday or today."

I looked at my phone. No cell service.

"Let's head back," Ryder suggested. "Once we get to the marina, I'll give Ernie a call."

"Do you know him?" I asked as Ryder carried me back to the boat.

"I do. His older brother, Kent, and I are friends."

The ride back toward Shipwreck Island was accomplished in silence. Once we arrived at the marina, Ryder thanked Nick and gave him some money for the gas he'd used to ferry us to the island. Ryder called Ernie, who didn't answer, so he called Kent, who told him that Ernie had mentioned heading over to Topsail Beach for a party. Luckily, Topsail Beach was only a short drive from the marina, so Ryder and I headed in that direction.

When we arrived at the beach, we found a group of young men and women, drinking near a large bonfire. It appeared to be a younger crowd, but Ryder recognized a few individuals who pointed us in the direction they'd last seen Ernie.

"Ernie," Ryder said once we found him smoking pot with a group of his peers.

"Hey, Ryder. What's up? Wanna hit?" he offered him his pipe.

"No, thanks. I'm looking for Sam. Have you seen him?"

Ernie seemed to be struggling to focus. He looked like he was totally smashed. "Yeah. This afternoon. The guys and I went waterskiing. We stopped to party on Horseshoe Island, and Sam was there. Not on the island, but in a boat."

"Boat?" I asked.

"Looked like Carson's boat. I'm not sure why Sam was in Carson's boat since it looked like he might have been there on official police business. He had on his uniform, and the boat he was in was tied up to another boat. A fishing boat. I remember thinking the guys in the fishing boat might have been poaching since that whole area is a marine preserve."

"Did you speak to him?" Ryder asked.

"No. I waved, but then one of the guys from the fishing boat joined Sam on his boat, and then both boats took off. Didn't see them again after that."

"Can you describe the fishing boat?"

He paused.

To be honest, he was so baked I figured any description he gave would be questionable, but questionable was better than nothing.

"It was white with a blue stripe, but to be honest, I wasn't really paying all that much attention to it."

"Outboard?"

He paused and then nodded. "Seems like. Cuddy cabin and a wench. Seemed to be outfitted for professional use."

"Do you remember anything about the men he was talking to?"

He slowly shook his head. "The guy who climbed onto his boat was an old dude. Brown skin and hair. Didn't really notice the others."

"How many men did you see?" Sam asked.

Ernie shrugged. "Three or four, I guess. Look, man, I'm sorry I can't be more specific, but I didn't know anyone was going to ask me about it, so I didn't pay all that much attention."

"Yeah, I get it." Ryder took Ernie's wallet out of his pocket and handed it to him. "I found this on the beach at Horseshoe Island."

"Dude. I didn't even know I lost it. I guess it must have fallen out of the pocket of my backpack when I pulled out my bottle of tequila."

"If you think of anything else, call me. I'll text you my number."

Ernie slipped his wallet into his pocket and then took a hit on his pipe. "Mermaid," he said. "The cabin of the boat had a mermaid on the side. Her tail was blue like the stripe."

Figuring we'd gotten about as much out of Ernie as we were likely to, we headed back to Ryder's truck.

"Now what?" I asked.

"I think it might be time to call Buford. Based on what we've been able to dig up, it really is beginning to sound as if Sam might be in trouble."

I called Quinn and filled her in while Ryder called Sam's deputy. In retrospect, we probably should have called Buford sooner, but I think Ryder and I both thought that if we looked around a bit, we'd be able to track Sam down. Maybe the boat he'd borrowed had broken down or run out of fuel. Maybe he was following a clue and had lost track of time. Maybe there was something going on between Sam and Quinn that Ryder and I simply didn't know about, and maybe he'd changed his mind about meeting her. There were explanations for Sam not meeting up with Quinn that didn't involve a violent end, but the more we discovered, the more convinced we both were that a violent end might actually be the case.

Chapter 13

Buford asked Ryder and me to meet him at the Hidden Harbor sheriff's office once we'd gotten ahold of him. Technically, today had been his day off since he would be working the next three days while Sam was off, but given the situation, he was happy to come in. We explained everything that was going on. The first thought he had was to find Sam's phone and truck. Ryder mentioned that Ernie had told us that Sam had probably borrowed Carson's boat, so Buford called him to confirm this fact. As it turned out, Carson was out of town but had been fine with Sam borrowing his boat, so he'd called down to the marina and asked the harbormaster to give Sam access to the boat. As for the key, Carson had told Sam where to find his extra key, which he'd hidden in his garage. Given the fact that we knew that in order for Sam to access Carson's boat, he had to go to the marina on the south shore rather than the marina where both

Ryder and Nick kept their boats, we all headed in that direction.

I called Quinn and filled her in as Ryder drove us to the south end of the island.

"I hate that I can't be there," she said.

"I know. And if I was the one stuck in San Francisco, I'd be frantic as well. But there really isn't anything you can do. There isn't anything any of us can do except continue to search."

"I found someone with a private chopper who's willing to bring me to the island. It will be expensive, and I'll have to come back for Jessica's car when this is all over, so I was waiting to hear from you before committing, but I can't just sit here. Can you pick me up in that big meadow where they usually set up the carnival in a couple of hours? It might be less. I'll have to call you with an exact time."

"Why not just land at the airport?"

"The guy I found isn't exactly on the up and up. Apparently, he's had some problems with his license and isn't allowed to land or take off at either the airport on this side or the airport on Shipwreck Island. But we worked that all out. So, will you pick me up?"

"Of course," I answered. "But are you sure you want to fly over the ocean in a helicopter, piloted by a man who's been banned from at least two airports?"

"I'm sure. I'm going to call him back now. I'll call you with an ETA."

"Okay. I'll see you later."

After I hung up, I told Ryder what Quinn had planned. He looked as unhappy about the whole thing as I was, but we both knew that once Quinn set her mind to something, there was no stopping her.

As predicted, Sam's truck was at the marina on the south shore. And as expected, Sam and the boat he borrowed, were nowhere to be found.

"So, now what?" I asked.

"I'm going to have the phone company ping his phone, although I suspect it's turned off or destroyed," Buford said.

I suspected the same thing, especially given the fact that the phone didn't even ring. It simply went straight to voicemail, but any tiny piece of information at this point would provide a lead, which at the moment, was something we were seriously short of. I kept thinking about what Ernie had said about someone joining Sam in his boat before both boats left Horseshoe Island. Assuming the man who joined Sam was one of the bad guys in this story, which would explain why Sam hadn't so much as called anyone, the only conclusion I could come up with was that by this point, he was probably dead. That wasn't an option I could really deal with.

A few minutes later, Buford received a text with an address on the north shore. "It looks like we found Sam's phone."

"Great," Ryder said. "Hopefully, Sam is with it."

At least the location of the phone wasn't in the middle of the ocean, which I'd suspected might be the case less than a minute ago.

Buford picked up his phone to call the Sea Haven office with an update. After he connected, however, I noticed he did all the listening and none of the talking.

"Okay," he eventually said. "I'm on it. Have them call me when they get here."

He hung up and looked at Ryder and me. "I'm afraid dispatch received a shots fired call just before I called in to speak to them about Sam's phone. Sea Haven is sending two deputies over to help, but at this moment, I'm the only one here, so I have to respond."

"I understand," Ryder said. "You go and do that, and Kelly and I will start heading to the north shore. We'll call and let you know what we find when we get there."

Buford looked reluctant to let us go, but I sensed he wanted to find Sam as much as we did. After making us both promise to simply check out the situation and not to engage should we find that Sam had been compromised by the man Ernie saw him speed away from Horseshoe Island with, he finally agreed to our plan.

"For the first time, I realize how inadequate it is for Hidden Harbor to only have two officers assigned to this entire side of the island," I said to Ryder as we sped north once again.

"Sam has been trying to talk the county into a third officer for the Hidden Harbor office for a year, but in their opinion, two is adequate, and it really hasn't been a problem in the past. Sam and Buford trade-off to give each other downtime, and the Sea Haven office is always happy to send someone over if there is a need. The amount of time it takes to get from Sea Haven to Hidden Harbor, however, can be a problem during an emergency situation. I suspect after this, Sam will have some fuel to add to his argument."

We were halfway to the north shore when I got a text from Quinn. "Darn," I said. "I forgot about

Quinn. We're supposed to pick her up on the south shore in twenty minutes."

"That's not going to happen," Ryder said. "Call Carrie. It's late and she probably already went to bed, but call anyway. If we can get ahold of her, she can pick Quinn up."

I did as Ryder suggested. He was correct in the fact that Carrie had already gone to bed, but once I explained the situation, she assured me that she was happy to get up and get dressed to meet Quinn. I then texted Quinn back and let her know about the change in plans.

"Do you think he's okay?" I asked. "Sam, I mean. Is it even possible that he has simply disappeared from the face of the earth yet is perfectly fine?"

Ryder snaked his right hand out until it met my left hand across the seat. He interlaced his fingers with mine and gave them a squeeze. "I think at this point, we have to assume that it is totally possible he's fine. It's really the only option open to us at this point. If he's not, we'll deal with it, but for now, we're heading north to rescue our friend who is waiting for us to do just that."

"Yeah. You're right. Sam's a smart guy. I'm sure he's managing whatever situation he's gotten himself into."

Ryder made the drive from the south shore to the north shore in record time. When we arrived at the address Buford had provided, we immediately noticed a private dock with Carter's boat tied up to it. The house associated with the dock was dark, so Ryder and I slowly made our way to the boat. A quick look around inside provided us with two new clues. The first clue was the phone we found tucked between the cushions of the long seat along the back of the boat. When Ryder turned it on, he saw that a text had been typed out but not sent. The text was to Buford, and the message simply said Dragon Cove.

"Maybe he was trying to tell Buford where the men he was with were taking him," I said.

"That's as good a bet as any. Dragon Cove is on this end of the island, about five miles east of here. There's a nice deepwater cove to anchor in, and an old boathouse that hasn't been in use for decades. It'd be a good place to hide something."

"Or someone," I finished his thought.

Ryder texted Buford and let him know about the boat, the phone, and the unsent text. He also shared the second clue with him, a length of rope about three feet long that appeared to be soaked in blood. Hopefully, it wasn't Sam's blood, but at this point, it made sense to operate under the assumption that Sam was alive, yet injured when he was last in the boat.

Buford texted Ryder back and informed him that the shots fired call was an active situation. A man with a gun, who'd had too much to drink, had taken his girlfriend hostage in one of the vacation rentals on the island. The guys who'd been on their way over from Sea Haven were headed to his location to help with the situation, so at least for the time being, we were on our own.

"I'll text Carrie and tell her where we're headed," I offered. "You know that once Quinn lands on the island, she is going to want to be part of this, and to be honest, we need her. She's used to this sort of thing. She'll keep a level head, and she'll know what to do should we catch up with the men who have Sam."

"Aren't you the one who used to be FBI?"

"I was, but I never so much as left the building. Given what I learned about Quinn the night we snuck onto Montgomery Island, I know that she has the skill set that will come in handy in a situation like this. If Buford and the others are going to be delayed, we're going to need her."

When Ryder and I arrived at Dragon Cove, we found the blue and white fishing boat Ernie had seen anchored in the bay. There was a rubber dingy on the beach, which I assumed had brought the men associated with the shadows that could be seen through the slats of the old boathouse to the shore.

"So, what now?" I whispered.

Ryder continued down the road, pulling off the pavement only after we'd rounded a corner, putting us out of sight of both the boat and the beach. "I'm going to text Buford," he said, "and let him know what we found. You text Quinn and tell her to have Carrie drive past the cove and pull off the road only after she sees my truck. We can't risk being seen from either the boat or the shore. We'll have to hide the vehicles and walk in on foot."

Once we'd each sent our texts, Ryder opened the driver's side door and slipped out of the truck.

"Aren't we going to wait for the others?" I asked.

"You are. I'm going to see if I can get a look inside the boathouse."

"You shouldn't go alone," I argued.

"Going alone really is the safest bet. Wait here for Quinn and Carrie. Keep an eye on your phone. I'll text you once I make my way back to the cove to let you know what I find."

I groaned in frustration when Ryder left, but I supposed it did make sense for him to go and me to wait for the others. Not that I was thrilled with waiting, but Ryder did make a good point when he said that there was a lesser chance of him being seen by anyone who might be watching the boathouse if there was only a single figure sneaking through the thankfully dark night.

My phone buzzed shortly after Ryder left. I answered.

"What's going on?" Quinn demanded.

"The boat Ernie saw tied up to the boat Sam borrowed this afternoon is anchored in Dragon Cove. It looks like there are people in the old boathouse. We noticed light and shadows, so they must have flashlights or lanterns. We suspect that men may still be on the boat as well. We are proceeding with caution."

"Did you see Sammy? Is he definitely there?" she demanded.

"We couldn't make out anyone specifically. Like I said, all we saw were shadows. Ryder went to check out the situation. I'm waiting for the two of you at the truck. Like I said in my text, continue past the cove. Don't even slow down. We don't want to draw anyone's attention. There's a sharp turn where the road heads back toward the south about a quarter of a mile down the road after the cove. Pull off the road. You should see Ryder's truck tucked into the trees just beyond the first little clearing."

"Okay," Quinn said. "We're on our way. I'm driving, so we should be there in about ten minutes."

She hung up, and I went back to waiting. I knew it was going to take Ryder a while to sneak through the wooded area toward the cove, approach the boathouse without being seen and peek inside, and then get back to where I was waiting, but it still seemed as if he'd been gone a long time. I opened my phone to compare the time of my text to Quinn before Ryder headed out with the current time and realized that very little time had passed after all.

Ryder still wasn't back by the time Quinn and Carrie arrived. After I greeted my friends, I texted him, letting him know that Quinn and Carrie had arrived and that we were all interested in his progress. He texted back, letting me know that he was on his way back, and we should sit tight. Easier said than done.

"I'm not just going to sit here," Quinn said after I read Ryder's text to her.

"I think we have to. Ryder will be here in a few minutes. He can fill us in on the situation, and we can figure out what to do from there."

I could see that Quinn was itching to do something, anything, but for now, she simply nodded and began pacing back and forth along the little ridge that separated the forested area from the road.

It only took a few minutes for Ryder to appear from the path that cut through the forested area.

"So, what'd you find?" Quinn demanded before he could even make it all the way back to the truck.

"Sam is in the boathouse. He's tied up, and there's blood on his shirt, but he looks okay otherwise. There are two men with him. Both are armed, although neither seemed overly alert. I was able to sneak up to the double doors on the seaside of the building and push one of the doors open enough to take a peek inside, and they didn't seem to notice a thing."

"If you were on the seaside of the building, you would have been visible from the boat anchored offshore," I pointed out.

"That's true, but I figured the men wouldn't be watching the sea doors, whereas they would be watching the little door that opens onto the beach."

"So, what's the plan?" Quinn asked.

Ryder frowned. "I'm not sure. I called Buford and filled him in. He's in the middle of a tense situation himself and promised to call me back. I say we wait and see what he says."

"But Sam..." Quinn started to argue.

"Looked just fine. I didn't sense that he was in any immediate danger. If they wanted him dead, he'd be dead. Chances are they simply want him occupied until they are able to do whatever they're here on the island to do and make their getaway."

"I wish I had my gun," Quinn grumbled.

"You have a gun?" I asked, surprised by this fact, although I supposed knowing Quinn, I really shouldn't be.

"Of course, I have a gun. Don't you? You were in the FBI," she reminded me.

"I was in the FBI, but, as I keep reminding everyone, I worked as an analyst and not an operative, so no, I don't have a gun."

"Based on what Ernie remembered, it sounded like there were four men in all," Ryder pointed out. "I only saw two in the boathouse, which means the other two are still on the boat or they are on the island taking care of whatever business they're in the area to take care of. No one is going to make a move until we hear from Buford; gun or no gun."

"Ryder's right," I said. "The best thing we can do for Sam at this point is to wait."

Luckily, we didn't have long to wait. Buford called to let us know the standoff was over. The man who'd been holding his girlfriend hostage had been apprehended. One of the men from the Sea Haven office was taking him in for booking while Buford and the other Sea Haven deputy were on their way north to help us with our situation. Buford instructed Ryder to wait and not to approach the cove again until he arrived. Quinn made a lot of noise about getting a peek for herself, but in the end, she stayed put with the rest of us. I figured Buford and the deputy with him had guns, which none of us currently had access to, so if they wanted us to wait so they could storm in and save the day, then that was exactly what I was going to let them do.

Of course, storming in might have been a reality that only made sense in my mind. What really happened was that Buford and the deputy from Sea Haven, a man named Ben, quietly made their way around to the back of the boathouse while Ryder drove his truck right up to the front of the building. When the men went out the front door to confront Ryder, Buford and Ben snuck in the back. They untied Sam, gave him a gun, and then all three men dealt with the two men who'd been holding Sam, while Ryder, who'd stayed in his truck the entire time, pulled safely away. Once everyone was disarmed, the two men who'd been holding Sam were loaded into Ben's car and taken south for booking.

"So what about the other two men?" I asked after Sam joined Ryder, Quinn, Carrie, and me in the forest near where we'd parked.

"They left to meet a man named Tyson. Buford and I are going to wait here for them to come back. I want the four of you to go home."

"But..." Quinn started.

"This is not a negotiation. If you don't leave, I'll have to arrest you for interfering in an ongoing investigation."

Quinn started to speak again. Sam put a finger over her lips.

"Please," he said. "Buford and I have this. Really. The other two guys don't know I'm free or that their buddies have been arrested. We have the element of surprise on our side. We're the cops, and you all are the civilians, so please wait for me at home and let me do my job."

Surprisingly, Quinn agreed after demanding to see the injury that had bloodied his shirt. Most of the blood had come from a single stab wound to his side that had stopped bleeding hours ago as well as the raw skin around his wrists where he'd been tied up. He actually did seem fine, and I, for one, was inclined to do as he asked.

"Counter proposal," Quinn said. "You and Buford head back to the boathouse to wait for the other two men, and the rest of us will wait here, safely out of the way."

"You'd be safer at home," Sam pointed out.

"True, but you don't really know what is going to happen. You might need us."

Sam hesitated.

"I have an extra gun in the trunk of my car," Buford said. "It might not be a bad idea to have backup just in case."

Sam frowned and then answered. "Okay. But if we get into trouble, you call Ben and tell him what's going on. The last thing we need is for any of you to get hurt."

We agreed to Sam's plan, which meant that the endless waiting would start anew. At least I had Ryder, Quinn, and Carrie here with me this time, which actually made the wait bearable until we heard the shots.

Chapter 14

The five minutes it took for us to make our way to the boathouse and to ascertain that it had been Sam who had shot one of the two men they'd been waiting for after they returned and pulled a gun on the two officers they found waiting for them were some of the longest minutes of my life. The man who'd been shot wasn't seriously wounded, but Buford still took him to the hospital in Sea Haven to be checked out before heading to jail while Sam took the other man straight to the holding cell in Hidden Harbor. Initially, neither man was talking, but it turned out that Sam had been able to get the kidnapper in his possession to spill the beans after he pointed out that he already had most of the story, so it made sense to cooperate in exchange for a chance at a lighter sentence. Once he had his confession, Ben showed up to transport the man to Sea Haven as well, and while he was at it, he convinced Sam to go to the hospital to have his stab wound and wrists looked at and cleaned up.

"So, the four men in the blue and white boat are connected to a drug cartel that is based south of the border?" Carrie asked Quinn who'd spoken to Sam. After our long night, we'd all slept in until noon. Once everyone woke up, we gathered on the outdoor deck to share a late brunch and catch each other up on what we knew and what we'd learned.

"That's what Sam said," Quinn confirmed as she ran a finger absentmindedly around the top of her coffee mug. "I spoke to him just before he left for Sea Haven to work out the details for the transfer of the four men to the larger jail on the mainland. He was able to find out that Veronica had unwisely let it be known that she had opiates to sell, which somehow managed to get the attention of the cartel that controls most of the opiate trade in this part of California. Of course, she didn't really have anything other than a few plants, which the cartel wouldn't even have bothered with had they known the truth, but unfortunately for her, she talked a good talk she couldn't quite support to get them there and ended up dead in the ocean."

"So it was these men who tossed her into the sea?" I asked.

"According to Sam," Quinn answered, "Veronica arranged to meet the men about half a mile offshore. Once she boarded their boat, the man she'd hired to ferry her out to the boat took off. Of course, once she actually had the attention of the men she tried to sell the plants to, they realized she'd overstated what she actually had to offer in order to gain an audience, and they tossed her overboard."

"I wonder why the guy who ferried her out to the boat didn't say something when she turned up dead," Carrie asked.

"I imagine he didn't want to get involved," Quinn answered. "But Sam is pretty sure that an anonymous tip he got, which led to his tracking down the blue and white fishing boat anchored off Horseshoe Island, probably came from the man who dropped Veronica off."

I supposed that made sense. Who else would know she'd met up with the men?

"So once Sam gets there to talk to the men in the fishing boat, the men grab him," Carrie said. "I guess I understand that to a point, but why were the men still hanging around? Veronica lured them to Shipwreck Island over a week ago. It seems they would have taken off long before this."

"According to Sammy," Quinn answered, "they just happened to pick up a new piece of information while they were here that they wanted to follow up on."

"What sort of information?" I asked.

"It seems that there's been some movement in the drug trade in San Francisco, and apparently one of the major players in the whole thing has a home here on the island. I guess the men decided to stay around for a few days as long as they were already here and get to the bottom of some of the rumors that had been making their way south for months. The man who they believed was in charge of the group they suspected of infringing on their territory was found dead in his island home this morning."

"So that probably means that the two men who were initially gone when we found Sam were most likely busy killing this man," I said.

"Talk about complicated." Carrie leaned back in her chair, tucking her feet up beneath her.

"It is complicated," Quinn agreed. "And, as it turns out, it appears to be a story deserving of my talent. I'm meeting up with Sam later so we can discuss the matter. I told him I wouldn't print anything I found out while working with him during my visit to the island, but at the time, we were talking about the case of the missing girls. After we spoke, we both agreed, in theory at least, that the story about the drug cartel and the changes taking place in the control of the drug trade in the Bay Area is worth writing about."

"So, Sam is okay?" I asked. "Physically, I mean. It looked like he'd lost a lot of blood."

"He's fine," Quinn answered. "He did manage to get a lot of blood, which should have been on the inside, all over his shirt, but the knife wound was cleaned up at the hospital, and no major organs were damaged."

"Well, I'm just glad everything worked out," Carrie said. "It seemed to be pretty touch and go for a while."

Quinn got up and refilled her coffee while I polished off the last of the omelet Carrie had made. It was nice to be able to simply sit and relax with my friends after the stressful night we'd had. Ryder had to work today, but he promised to come by when he got off. Quinn had mentioned meeting up with Sam. It looked like we were about to bail on poor Carrie again. I'd be glad when Nora arrived tomorrow to even things out for a bit.

"Is Nora still coming back tomorrow?" I asked since I was thinking about it, and we really hadn't discussed the status of her plans for a few days.

"Actually, she's coming this afternoon. Nora and Matt are planning a vacation, and Matt wanted to get back to have time to tackle any work he needed to get done before they left."

"That's great," I said. "I'm looking forward to seeing her."

"Me too, but it sounded like she might not stay as long as she originally planned. In fact, it sounded like she'd only be here a few days, but she did mention that she planned to go to the regatta with us on Sunday, and she wanted to be here for a meet up with Peggy if we're able to arrange such a thing," Carrie answered.

"I haven't had a chance to talk to Sam about it, but I will," I said.

"You know," Carrie said, stretching her legs out in front of her after untucking them from beneath her body. "We, as a group, actually managed to accomplish a lot in just a few weeks. I'll admit that by *we*, I mostly mean Sam, but I feel like we all helped."

"Carrie's right," Quinn said. "Since we've been here, we've helped Sammy track down Peggy and Cherry. We know what happened to Veronica, at least ultimately, although there are some missing pieces, and I don't suppose we'll ever know why she originally left or who she left with. We also know what happened to Hillary Denton, thereby solving her missing persons case, and I was able to find Grace before she'd been missing too long. I'd say we did okay for ourselves."

I lifted my champagne glass. "To us."

Everyone clinked the glassware for whatever beverage they were drinking.

"I guess the only missing girl we don't know anything about is Gina Baldwin," Carrie said.

"Gina was listed as a runaway," I reminded her. "Chances are she did just that. The only reason her file even made it into the limelight was because of Sam's theory about the missing girls being linked, which turned out not to be true."

"That's true," Quinn agreed. "If not for the fact that Sam decided to look for Peggy which led to him narrowing in on Gina's file he probably would have just filed it and been done with it."

"It is odd that none of the girls actually were linked to Peggy," Carrie said. "Sam did seem to have a theory that made sense."

"It was a good theory," I agreed. "Although if you stop and look at what really happened you'll see that it was Sam who made everything fit in the first place. He specifically went looking for missing teenagers with blond hair and blue eyes. When he came across a gap in this theory he forced a substitution, like with the situation with two thousand and ten where there wasn't an obvious candidate to fill the role." I took a sip of my drink. "I guess in the end though it was Sam's theory that really opened up the investigation and probably led to us finding Peggy which we may never have otherwise done."

"So yay for Sam," Carrie said.

"Yay for Sam," I agreed. "So I guess if Nora isn't staying long, our camping trip up the mountain is off."

"I guess," Carrie agreed. "But maybe it will work out to see Peggy, and even if it doesn't, I guess we can all get together and share memories around the campfire." Carrie looked at Quinn. "You haven't mentioned how long you plan to stay."

She shrugged. "You have the house for another two weeks. I guess I'll stay until the rental is up."

"I've decided to stay here on the island," I informed Quinn since I hadn't had a chance to. "I'm moving into Carrie's guest room temporarily, and if things work out, I'll get my own place at some point. We both hope you'll consider coming back for Christmas."

She furrowed her brow. "You're staying?"

I nodded. "I just decided yesterday, so I didn't have a chance to tell you."

She looked from me to Carrie. I wasn't sure what she was thinking, but she seemed to have a wistful expression. Eventually, she spoke. "I'd like to come back for Christmas. I might even come for Thanksgiving and stay clear through until the New Year."

"Really?" I asked. "I mean, that would be awesome, but you don't normally like to take so much time off work."

"Yes, that is true, or at least it has been in the past, but I've been thinking about things since I've been here. I think it might be time to reevaluate the amount of time I spend working compared to the amount of time I spend living my life."

I was happy to hear her say as much. The girl really did work much too hard.

"I'm hoping Jessica comes home for the holidays, but if she doesn't, which given my move, is likely, you can stay in her room if you want," Carrie offered.

Quinn smiled a small knowing smile. "Thanks, but if I come to the island over the holidays, I'll stay with Sammy. He's already offered, and to be honest, I've thought of little else since he made that offer."

I glanced at Carrie, and she smiled in return. Maybe, in the long run, I wouldn't be the only friend moving to the island.

Chapter 15

The three days that followed our brunch on Friday had been memorable, to say the least. Nora showed up as promised on Friday afternoon. She looked happy and refreshed, yet admitted that she and Matt had a lot of work to do on a marriage that had deteriorated without either of them realizing it. She shared that it wasn't until the two of them were forced to spend time as couple dissecting the decisions they'd made along the way, that they were able to understand how things had eventually gone so wrong.

On Friday evening, the four of us made dinner together, but after Nora's long drive from Mendocino, and the long night Carrie, Quinn, and I'd had the night before, we all agreed to turn in early. We knew Saturday was going to be a long and emotional day, which would require us to be at our best since Sam had succeeded in arranging a visit between Peggy and Carrie, Nora, Quinn, and myself. I really hadn't allowed myself to hope the get together we sought with Peggy would ever be a reality, but Sam spoke to Wilson on our behalf, and it just so happened that Wilson had planned a trip to the island to spend the afternoon with one of his lady friends. He'd managed to convince Peggy that she'd be perfectly safe meeting with us on his yacht while he was away.

It might have been slightly better if he'd been able to convince her to come here to the house, but she really had suffered a depth of emotional damage that left her with serious trust issues, so I was happy for any sort of gathering she might agree to.

Sam had shared that Peggy seemed to feel safe on the yacht, knowing that Wilson, who she seemed to be anchored to in some way, would be back shortly. I was certain she'd be nervous about the meetup, so I spoke to the others, and we agreed to take things slow and easy. We'd allow her to share what she wanted but wouldn't push if she preferred us to do the talking. We hoped that over time, we'd be able to get her to trust us the way she trusted Wilson.

Sam and Ryder accompanied us in the boat to meet Wilson's yacht, but they both agreed to wait for us in Ryder's boat, so we could have alone time with our friend. When we arrived, we were ushered aboard the yacht and then shown to a dining area where a virtual feast had been set out. I had to hand it to Wilson, he'd really seemed to go out of his way to a make things comfortable for all of us. I will admit that things were awkward at first, and Peggy looked like all she really wanted to do was run and hide, but as the day progressed, and we shared memories with Peggy as well as stories about our lives, she began to relax. Telling her about Kayla had been tough for all of us, but by the time Wilson returned, and we were ready to leave, we'd been able to get Peggy to agree to another meal together in the future.

Sam and Ryder joined the four of us for a meal Saturday night. The guys didn't stay late. I think they knew that with Nora leaving in a few days, our time together was limited, but I think they wanted to turn in early too since tomorrow was the big race.

On Sunday, Carrie, Nora, Quinn, and I met up with Cliff's wife and Nina's fiancé. The best place to view the race was Topsail Beach, and Carrie had arrived early to stake out a space for our group in the best viewing spot on the beach. Of course, as I knew they would, Ryder's team won. It was a close race with them only managing to squeeze ahead in the last seconds before crossing the finish line, but I suspect that had been their strategy all along. After the race was over, we all partied on the beach, drinking and sharing stories of past races around the campfire. The longer I sat under the moonlit sky listening to stories shared by friends old and new, the more certain I was that staying on Shipwreck Island was the right thing to do.

After a busy weekend full of friends and activities, Monday had been reserved for just the four of us. We'd made a huge brunch together, and then we hiked part of the way up the mountain. Not to the top as we'd planned at one point, but far enough that we all felt satisfied with the effort the way one should when they've conquered a difficult feat. After we returned from hiking, we showered and then headed out to dinner, but it was the gathering around the campfire on the beach after dinner that really topped off this visit for me.

"I have something for Carrie," I said once we were all gathered around the fire with our glasses of wine.

"For me?" Carrie said, truly surprised. "Whatever for? It's not my birthday."

"I know." I handed her a wrapped package. "But you did go to a whole lot of trouble to bring us all together, and you are the one who keeps us connected even when we aren't together. I love you. I wanted to do something for you."

Carrie slowly opened the package and gasped. "Oh my. Would you look at this!"

"A photo album?" Nora asked.

"Not just a photo album," I said. "This is the album of us: The Summer Six. After I got here, I found old photos that Kayla had left behind in the secret compartment of her desk as well as old journals I'd left behind in the secret compartment of mine. I had copies made of some of the best photos, and I transferred passages from my journals to scrapbook paper to fill things out. I wasn't sure at first if it would all come together, but I have to say that I think it turned out rather nice."

"It's perfect," Carrie said, tears streaming down her face.

I leaned over and hugged her. She hugged me back, and then looked through the book, stopping to comment on several of the photos while we all looked over her shoulders. The photos started early and spanned more than a decade, right up to that last summer together when we were eighteen. I felt like between Kayla's photos and my journal entries, it really was the story of us.

"Oh, gosh. Look at us here," Carrie pointed to a photo of the six of us when we were around seven or eight. "I forgot Quinn's hair was so long when we were young." She looked up and smiled at Quinn. "I love the short hair you sport now, but I do miss those pigtails."

"Too hard to keep long pigtails clean when I'm wading through muck up to my waist," she pointed out. "Besides, if I had hair that long now, I'd probably get it tangled up in my chute when I jump. Short is the only way to go when you live the lifestyle I do."

Carrie's expression became serious. "I know what you do is dangerous, but I guess I never stopped to consider how dangerous."

Quinn smiled at her, gently putting a hand on her shoulder. "No need to worry. I'm careful, and I know what I'm doing. Besides, not all my stories require jumping into enemy territory. At least half the stories I do are a lot more boring and tedious than they are dangerous."

I wasn't sure that was true since Quinn seemed to love covering wars and uprisings, but I supposed she did cover her share of white-collar and political stuff as well.

"Oh, look here's one with Matt before we even started dating," Nora said, pointing to a photo on the page. "I guess he was around fifteen. I forgot what a good-looking guy he was even back then. No wonder I fell hard the first time I saw him at the harvest fair."

"I remember that," Carrie said. "We were in line for the tilt-o-whirl, and he tried to cut in line. You told him in no uncertain terms that cutting wasn't allowed, at which point he smiled and winked at you and you let him into the line in front of you. I think that was the beginning of what was to come, even though you didn't actually start dating until the following summer."

"I was only up for the weekend when we saw him at the festival," Nora reminded Carrie. "I didn't even know his name at that point, or if he was local or a visitor. I wasn't sure I'd see that cute boy with the big brown eyes ever again until my family came back for the summer, and he was here, waiting for me just where I'd left him." She paused as if remembering a memory she chose not to share. "You know, Matt told me that his family almost went to Europe that summer. I shudder to think about how different my life would be if they hadn't come to the island, and Matt and I hadn't gotten together."

"But Matt was your fated love, and fate always wins out," Carrie said with a tone of regret in her voice. She paused for a moment. "I thought Carl was my fated love, but I was wrong. Since we've split up, I've actually wondered if I hadn't met and discarded my real soulmate while chasing around after a man who was never going to be worthy of my love."

"If you have actually met your soulmate, yet missed your chance, it seems to me that your paths will cross again," I said.

She smiled. "I hope so."

Carrie turned the page to a photo of the six of us sitting on a blanket at the beach when we were probably around fifteen or sixteen. Ryder and his buddy at the time, Dillon, were hanging out in the background with those dang Super Soakers they used to torture us with. They looked so young, and somehow looking at ten-year-old Ryder, in contrast to fifteen-year-old me, abruptly brought home the difference in our ages.

"Ryder doesn't still have that dang water gun, does he?" Quinn teased. "He was such a pest, always following us around, playing tricks on us, and spying on us even after we'd told him to leave us the heck alone."

"Ryder has moved past the pesky brother phase," Carrie spoke up. "I'd never have survived my divorce without him."

"I know," Quinn admitted. "I was just teasing. Seeing these photos just brought back memories of that little kid that served as a thorn in our sides for years, but he's turned out to be someone really special." She peeked over Carrie's shoulder. "I guess we didn't really hang out with Sammy, so there probably aren't any photos of him in this book."

"Actually, there is one," I said. I looked at Carrie, "Turn to the back, maybe three pages from the end.

The page had a photo of Sam, who'd been seventeen when I was fourteen, and Quinn was fifteen. He was sitting on his Harley, wearing the same leather jacket he still owned.

"My, my, my," Quinn said. "How did I not remember what a babe he was?"

"You thought he was a pest," I reminded her. "Maybe he was a pest, in a different way than Ryder was a pest, but he had a thing for you even back then, and he seemed to show up wherever we were a lot more often than might normally be explained by chance."

She reached over Carrie's shoulder and ran a finger over his face. "Guess I forgot about that." She took a deep breath, her face softening. "He's turned out to be exactly the sort of guy I'd be looking for if, in fact, I was looking for a guy."

"I know you travel a lot with your job, but you know you are always welcome here," Carrie reminded her. "I'm here, Kelly is going to stay, at least for the time being, and most importantly, if you spend more time on the island, maybe you can explore this thing with Sam and see where, if anywhere, it might end up."

She nodded. "I am getting to the point in my life where the urge to settle down is settling in, so maybe." She glanced at the photo again. "I know I used to complain about Sammy hanging around all the time when we lived here as kids, but if I'm perfectly honest, I had a pretty big crush on him even back then. I would never have admitted it even to myself, but I remember this feeling of gladness whenever he'd show up. Of course, I wasn't going to let any guy get in the way of the plans I had for my life — but now — maybe."

I'd missed Quinn a lot over the years. I hoped she would continue to come around. Maybe one day, she'd even want to stay.

Carrie turned back toward the middle of the book where she'd left off. My eyes settled on an image of Kayla and me. I seemed to remember that Carrie had snapped it. We were probably around twelve. We both wore long braids, and our tanned skin was free of makeup, even the mascara we'd both begun to wear when we were around thirteen. I felt my throat tighten as I struggled with my emotions. She should be here. Somehow, it seemed all wrong that she wasn't. She would have loved this so much, spending time with friends who'd helped to mold us into the people we were today.

Quinn, who stood next to me as we looked over Carrie's shoulders, reached out and took my hand in hers. She didn't say anything as she wound her fingers through mine, but I knew that she'd been focused on the same photo I was. After Kayla died, I'd felt so alone in my grief, but here on the island with people who loved her almost as much as me, I felt less alone than I'd felt for a very long time.

The four of us continued to sit by the campfire, sharing memories late into the night. We shared things that night that we'd never shared with the others in the past. I supposed it was the wine loosening our tongues, or the photos and the vivid recollections of a life that seemed so far in the past yet somehow still within our grasps. We talked about both Peggy and Kayla, and what they'd meant to each of us. We'd laughed, we'd cried, we allowed ourselves to grieve, and then to find joy in the memories that were left when our grief was spent. By the time the fire finally burnt down to ash, the bond of friendship the four of us had forged as children had been renewed. I knew, in my heart, that while I'd always grieve the fact that I wouldn't fade into the sunset with Kayla as planned, I did have people in my life who'd be with me until the sun met the sea for the final time.

Epilogue

Ryder moved up behind me, wrapping his arms around my waist. "Penny for your thoughts," he whispered into my ear before trailing a row of kisses down my neck.

I continued to stare out the window of the boathouse at the sunny morning and gently rolling sea. "I was thinking about how much I am both looking forward to and dreading today before you distracted me with whatever it is you're doing to my neck."

He stopped what he was doing and turned me so that we were facing one another. "I'm sorry about the distraction. Do you want to talk about it?"

I shrugged. "I'm not sure what there is to say. On one hand, I'm so excited that Quinn, Nora, and Matt are all going to be here for Thanksgiving this year, that I can barely contain my happiness but on the other hand…"

"This is your first Thanksgiving without Kayla, and you're missing her," he finished for me.

I nodded, tears gathering behind my lids as I stared into his blue eyes. "She was in the hospital last year. I barely remember the holidays. I think I forced them out of my consciousness since thinking about a life of Thanksgivings and Christmases without Kayla was overwhelming." I took a breath and then continued. "I know she wouldn't want me to be sad. And I don't want to be sad. And in a way, I'm not. I have you and Carrie, and Quinn and Sam, and Nora and Matt. I have people I love, who love me in return. The thought of sharing the next month with you and establishing our own holiday rituals that I hope we will repeat for years to come brings me more joy than I can even describe. I guess I just felt the need to take a moment and remember."

"I get that," Ryder pulled me toward his chest, wrapping his arms around me. "Do you want to be left alone?"

I shook my head. "Not really. It's hours until we need to pick Quinn up at the ferry terminal, and Matt and Nora meet us at Carrie's place. Let's take a walk and then have some breakfast. Carrie said she isn't planning to serve Thanksgiving dinner until around five."

Ryder put some distance between our bodies, leaned in to kiss me gently on the lips, and then headed toward the chair where he'd draped the sweatshirt he'd worn last night. I pulled mine on as well. It was warm for November, but there was a chill in the air that hinted that winter was just around the corner.

"So why isn't Sam picking Quinn up?" Ryder asked as we left the boathouse and walked out onto the sandy beach. "He's been yammering on and on for days about how happy he is that she's going to be here until after New Year's."

"Buford took the long weekend off to be with family, so Sam is covering. He's working a basic eight-hour day and then is going to be on call the rest of the time, so he'll just meet us at Carrie's."

"You do realize you always refer to the condo as Carrie's place even though you're both living there, don't you?"

"For now," I answered.

"Have you given more thought to moving in with me?" he asked.

"Actually, I have," I answered. I spent more nights at the boathouse than I did at the condo, so it made sense to move in with Ryder. "Jessica is going to be here next week, and Quinn is staying with Sam, so I want to give Carrie alone time with her daughter. I packed a bunch of my stuff to take to the boathouse today, so it looks like you're stuck with me for at least the next couple of weeks. I'll admit that I've been toying with the idea of moving to your place permanently, although I do enjoy having the occasional quiet evening with Carrie when it works out that I'm home on the same night that Glen isn't visiting, which admittedly is occurring less and less often."

"What's up with that anyway?" Ryder asked. "Are Carrie and Glen a couple now?"

I paused. "She hasn't labeled what they have as a romance, so I'm not going to go there, but he comes over at least four or five nights a week to have dinner and watch TV. Glen is a nice guy, who seems to like to do the same things Carrie likes to do. I think they fit. I'm not sure that Carrie is ready to jump into another relationship quite yet, but I'd be surprised if that isn't where they're heading."

"I like Glen," Ryder said, putting an arm around my shoulder as Baja took off after a colony of seagulls. "I've always liked him. Personally, I think he'd be good for Carrie."

"Me too," I agreed. "I really hope it works out for them."

I paused and thought about a dream that I'd had not all that long ago. It had been a cold and blustery day, but Ryder and I, and Carrie and Glen, and Quinn and Sam, and Nora and Matt were all on the beach, building a snowman out of sand. It doesn't snow on Shipwreck Island, but that doesn't mean we don't go all out for the holidays with tree lightings and festivals, and all the decorations and trimmings. One of the events held here on the island is a Christmas themed sandcastle contest. I'd been thinking about entering this year, which I supposed is where the fuel for the dream came from.

"I joined the committee overseeing the Christmas on the Island event," I informed him. "I understand you are likewise on the committee, but I didn't see you at the meeting today."

"I was actually meeting with the tree lighting committee today. I assume you were at the meeting for the festival in mid-December."

I nodded. "I wasn't sure I wanted to join the group when Carrie first mentioned it to me. I think she's been trying to help me feel settled, and in her own way, she seems to think that being part of the committee will help with that. I actually considered bowing out, but she really wanted me to do it, so I went."

"And?" he asked, caressing my palm with his finger as we walked hand in hand.

"And I had a blast. I only spent Christmas on the island a couple of times when I was a kid. We came every summer, but rarely between summers. But I remember the Christmas themed sandcastle competition and the parade down Main Street. I remember the festival and carolers. I remember the town feeling like something out of a movie. I remember being enchanted. To be honest, I'm looking forward to the holidays this year more than I've looked forward to them in a very long time."

"Me too." He grinned. "I may even allow you to help me with decorating the tree this year."

I laughed. "Is that supposed to be some sort of privilege?"

"Actually, it is. Baja and I have a tradition of decorating our tree — just the two of us. We never allow anyone to help. But this year, I think we might be willing to make an exception. For you, that is. No one else. Just you."

"I'm honored. And don't worry, I totally rock at tree decorating. I won't let the two of you down. I don't really have any decorations to contribute, but I'm sure you have that covered."

"We do," he confirmed.

I laid my head on his shoulder as we continued to stroll hand in hand. I closed my eyes, trusting him to lead the way as I focused on the water washing across my feet and the salty air as it caressed my cheek.

I'd come to Shipwreck Island as a broken woman, hoping to find a way to cope with a loss so great that it threatened to destroy me.

I'd come to Shipwreck Island in the hope of finding a way to deal with my anger and grief.

I'd come to Shipwreck Island, hoping to find solace in my darkest hour.

But somewhere along the way, between the pain and the healing, I'd found a way to go on living. I'd found hope, I'd found meaning, I'd found new relationships to fill the void, and most of all, I'd found a love so pure, I knew it would sustain me the rest of my days.

USA Today best-selling author Kathi Daley lives in beautiful Lake Tahoe with her husband Ken. When she isn't writing, she likes spending time hiking the miles of desolate trails surrounding her home. She has authored more than a hundred and fifty books in thirteen series. Find out more about her books at www.kathidaley.com

Made in the USA
Monee, IL
01 March 2021

61665624R00098